TWENTY-THREE
–
TWO WORLDS

TWENTY-THREE
–
TWO WORLDS

a novel
Karl Hiltner

TꙄMƎIИ K PRESS

HUDSON

Kniemst Press
Hudson, Ohio
www.karlhiltnerbooks.com

ISBN 979-8-9852154-0-3
Library of Congress Control Number: 2021923116

For Neptune, and the ships that brought me back.

Contents

Waves on waves break within me;
that sea sound in my ears, that
salt taste on my lips, that knowledge of
plankton and womb waters.

Rocking, breasts like ocean swells,
the sea emerges from our skin
like mountains emerging beyond the beach.

I lick your body, sucking salt,
and swim mouth open with the moon's tide,
till the sea, rising with white foam,
carries me to the beach.

Song of the Proterozoic
R.T.

Epilogue

i

Older than his three closest friends, at three hundred seventy-eight years of age, one third of his life had already passed, perhaps as much as one half, yet he hoped he would have a full thousand years to work and learn and develop and build, whether here on this planet or on the new world. He wondered what thoughts were in the minds of his friends. He knew that in many ways they did not share the emotional intensity of his passions, and perhaps because of this they had more balanced aspects to certain parts of their lives. There were so many things which generated no passion in him, or even preference, whether sexual, the surroundings in which he lived or worked, the food he ate, or the two children he had fathered during his five spousal assignments. For many of his basic needs he had no firm preference. For him it was work that drove his passion, and the end of work was the end of life. He felt a strange sense of hopelessness and emptiness at a time of hope for a second world, and the greatest migration in human history, like seeds that survived ocean crossings and planted themselves in new islands and continents of ages past. The age of man was poised after two billion years of life ascendancy to sail across an interplanetary emptiness to make another new, blue world.

He addressed the glowing screens suspended in front of him, surrounded by three dimensional representations of probabilities. He vowed to himself that his work not become an elegy to life on Earth, but instead the technology of a new birth which required an acceptance of the possibility of death, even the death of a planet in order to survive. And he imagined a tiny spacecraft as if ejaculated from the gravity of its own planet Earth, propelled upon the streaming exhaust tail of its rocket engine as it passed through the bounds of the Earth's atmosphere, ejected into space, coursing through the near perfect vacuum, the occasional trailing tail of a hydrazine thruster flight correction, the craft's only purpose to cross inhospitable space, enter the gaseous atmosphere of a new world, and implant itself onto the surface to establish new life.

The image of a new conception.

ii

We all live in at least two worlds, the present and the past, the human condition of all who live long enough to possess consciousness, and we all hope for a third, the future, but that is a world we can never achieve, for we are prisoners of the present. Our individual and personal connection to the past is tenuous and short-lived, and extends backwards only a generation or two or three, or if we are lucky enough, perhaps a fourth, if our consciousness was developed enough and we were old enough to remember the lap of a great-grandmother or great-grandfather, the sound of a voice, a song, or the bristle of a chin. We survive in the moment, the present that engulfs us, so that even the past is only a memory of the present past, an imperfect recollection, a confusion of faulty memories and things which we think have been said or done or seen, but become less distinct and sure with age, when eventually even memory of the past fades away. The record of DNA remains, however, within our twenty-three pairs of chromosomes, perhaps the only true evidence of the past, the source and record of all life; of change, of history, that each of us carries within us in every cell, the true fiber of our being, and of every living organism on Earth, and perhaps in the undiscoverable universe of space and time.

The present can start and stop, be suspended and brought to life again. It occurs in nature with simple life forms, or with the assistance of modern medical technology for even the most complex of human organisms.

Only a generation ago a virgin birth required a leap of faith without which it could not be understood or demonstrated. Yet now in every developed country on Earth in-vitro fertilized virgin births take place each day, while cryogenic vessels contain millions of bits of life suspended, in both male and female gamete, and fertilized blastocyst forms – life potential, and life begun, haploid and diploid life waiting to be awakened from their cryogenic suspense. There now exists more cryogenically preserved potential life than the number of lives that existed at the beginning of current recorded human history on Earth, a brief time span that if graphed the length of a single piece of paper compared to the four and a half billion years of our planet, would be only 1/100 the width of a human hair.

We will all continue to live in at least the two worlds of the present and the past, and increasingly in our mobile and mixed-up world we share life in different places and families, cities, countries, hemispheres – northern and southern, eastern and western, in the cacophony of languages in which we reside, worlds shared and worlds abandoned, creating new pasts out of the fabric of present lives.

Through it all and in spite of all change, the record remains in the DNA of our forty-six chromosomes in twenty-three pairs, inherited from each of the mothers and fathers that preceded us, the record of life past and of life present, which governs the life of our presence, and continues forever into a future which we shall individually never attain.

So perhaps the end is only the beginning, the epilogue the true prologue.

I
Wind

i

The immensity of space and time.

From deep within the 15 million degrees Kelvin temperature of the sun's thermonuclear core, energy particles collide for one hundred thousand years through the radiative zone before making their way to the 2 million K convective layer, a bubbling caldron of hot plasma and ionized gases, the convective movement of which creates a swirling magnetic field. The indescribable brightness blinds us as our sensors are not immune to the heat and destruction in our presence, and fills our entire perceived universe with a blinded perception of violence. Now we pass through the whiteness of the 5,800 K photosphere, and next into the red, hydrogen filled 4,600 K chromosphere. The suns massive gravity prevents the millions degree heat of the core, radiative, and convective zones from radiating beyond the cooler photosphere and pulls it back downwards in a red shift from the chromosphere. The gaseous plasma that is able to attain an escape velocity of six hundred kilometers per second, finally escapes the sun's surface and releases its heat – free from the sun's immense gravity – into the billowing 3 million K corona. It escapes and is blown off the surface of the chromosphere to become the streaming solar wind which will reach outward to the boundary of the solar system's heliosphere, beyond which lies the termination shock, the heliosheath, and the heliopause. Now we find ourselves at the edge of interstellar space.

Our G2V main-sequence star, a yellow dwarf visibly emanating a brilliantly white photosphere, is 4.6 billion years old, converting 600 million tons of hydrogen to 99% helium and 1% energy each second, impassively indistinguishable from the nearby Alpha Centauri A, and is almost halfway to its 10-billion- year life. It is only 1 of 100 billion stars in its galaxy, 25,000 light years from the core, and its voyage is a 250-million-year orbit around this galaxy, the Milky Way, while moving away from the other stars at 19 kilometers per second. Consuming the energy equivalence of 100 billion tons of dynamite per second, the sun holds 99.9% of the mass of its entire solar system.

We are only the tiniest speck of a speck, of a speck of a particle, of star dust.

In 5 billion years, when most of its hydrogen is consumed and the hydrostatic equilibrium of density and pressure can no longer contain the nuclear fusion of the core, the outer layers of our star will expand to engulf its first two planets and become an M2III red giant.

The collective speck of a speck that we collectively are has inhabited only the tiniest blip of time. Were a representative to travel from the sun, past the innermost planet to the outermost planet, through the orbits of the 8 planets and their 173 moons, and the 5 dwarf planets with their 8 moons, the successive backward glances would reveal the overwhelming heat and brightness of its sun gradually reduced to its own blip of a blip of light and heat from the boundary of the heliosphere, the boundary of illimitable space. Now from this distance of 94 Astronomical Units, fourteen billion kilometers, it is apparent only as the brightest star in our field of vision. Reduced to a point of light, it is still massive enough to capture us in perpetuity, cabled by its gravity. The end of our journey now finds us staring outward into the abyss of an impossible vastness, where the ancient light of distant worlds finally reaches our eyes across the cosmos, beyond which other worlds lay in darkness, distant enough from us so that their light will not yet reach us for countless eons.

ii

Far off, faintest light glinting off its MLI metallic surface, traveling at 7 kilometers per second relative to its distant star, the sun. Its frozen cargo as cold as the interplanetary space through which it glides silently on its timeless orbit, the Multi-Layered-Insulation draped across its surface shows tiny pitted marks as it sweeps the route of its path. It approaches silently as if lifeless, though inside the cryoprotectants have prevented intercellular ice crystals from forming within the stabilized and protected delicate cell membranes, powerful only in their latent energy and potential to create new life. A soundless sweeping by, silently rotating, cold, no emissivity of a heat source within, a frozen craft inside and out, only an imagined heat of potential, radiating nothing to space, receiving nothing in return through its blankets of metalized gold fabric, scrim, and beta cloth. It passes by silently, dark, the surface reflection of a 25 AU distant light source star effecting the tiniest glimmer on its surface, un-sun-like the faint illumination against its home in the distant expanse of space, still bound and captured by the distant star's gravity within the heliosphere. It travels a velocity only half of that which released it from the bounds of its source, so distant it flies from its origin. Its passage unseen, unheard, without communication – deaf, dumb, blind. A vanishing point in space, passed by and continuing on an endless journey, an infinite falling, receding unseen into the blackness of the solar system as it passes by, a horizonless dispassionate appearing and disappearing on each orbit of its illimitable potential.

The blackness of space and a temperature which only begins to approach that of absolute zero. The silence of the solar wind and a near complete vacuum except for the charged particles and dust which escaped the formation of the planets, a density so slight, that each one of the one-hundred-thousand-degree Celsius temperature solar wind particles can add insufficient heat to raise the temperature of the spacecraft's environment from that of the near absolute coldness of deep space. The interplanetary environment at the outer reaches of our solar system. Between the orbits of Uranus and Neptune this singular lifeboat orbits the distant sun, silently, in a millenniums old mission. There are no sounds here perceptible to the human ear even though the supersonic solar wind through which the craft sails will not slow to a subsonic velocity until it meets the termination shock at 94 AUs – ninety-four times the Earth's distance from the sun.

The solar wind of charged particles emitted from the violent surface of our sun streams outward through the heliosphere's cocoon of our solar system to where interplanetary space meets the realm of the interstellar. Here, at the termination shock, the solar wind slows to a subsonic speed. Beyond, at the heliopause, the solar wind is stopped by galactic cosmic rays pervasive throughout the galaxies of the universe. The solar wind and the cosmic rays of interstellar space now press against each other in equilibrium beyond the heliosphere of our sun, creating the turbulent boundary of the heliosheath. Like the buoyant, rolling surface of a child's giant soap bubble within which is contained our sun and our planets, undulating waves on the surface of this final boundary of our solar system press against the cosmic rays of interstellar space.

Our solar system, with the craft orbiting within, traverses onward and outward through space and time. It has already traveled in one form or another – from galactic gas clouds of primordial creation to the formation of its own sun and planets. Now it continues on, in its journey through fourteen billion years of a still expanding universe.

There are no ears here, no eyes, no sensory perception as we know it, only the premise of a capture at some future rendezvous and a possible resurrection. From the position of the singular orbit of this man-made satellite, the sun, still the brightest star in the sky at a distance of twenty-five astronomical units, casts only a gentle shadow on the surface of the craft. It rotates slowly and silently, surrounded by the continuous dome of stars of the Milky Way and other galaxies, and the strange and incomprehensible structures of intergalactic space; the baryonic matter of galaxy filaments, quasars, and the great walls of many megaparsecs and even billions of light years across in size which brighten the blackness beyond our own heliosphere. Sister planets of our own solar system appear only as stars of varying color with magnitudes greater than those of the nearest stars, the distances from the craft between one outer planet and seven inner planets being so vast within its own solar system. And the inner planets dance back and forth in the rhythm of billions of years, in conjunction and opposition to the sun's position in the orbital plane of our solar system, were the ancient, blind spacecraft able to look in the direction of the sun and view them.

If there were capable a backward glance from the craft toward this sun in the direction of the fourth planet, an almost imperceptible blip in its atmosphere would not be visible to the viewer, too subtle to be noticed with or without the naked eye. Silent and dispassionate, its frozen cargo suspended at minus two hundred degrees Centigrade, the craft continues on its journey of millenniums, unmoved by an event it is incapable to detect. Moving at twenty-four thousand kilometers per hour, it sails silently through interplanetary space, a patient voyager with or without an unknown hope of rescue in its emotionless, dispassionate, journey around the sun.

iii

Great masses of the atmosphere ejected into space propelled by the heat of a million suns. In the fraction of an instant the first molecules boiled to incandescence, then transmutation and escape velocity, followed in succession as the cascading effect began to consume nearly two quadrillion kilotons of the atmosphere which no longer pressed against the surface of the planet.

Hurricane forces of plasma and plasticized tornado vortexes scoured the invisible, odorless, tasteless gases from every surface, crevice, mountain, stream; imploded the space of every natural cave or architectural structure, flattened what did not implode, and ejected the radiating masses of stone, mountain, plains. Whole valleys which had been ejected to near space returned, now incandescent, through the roaring atmosphere to burn what remained on the surface with infrared radiance. The seas boiled, the immense sublimating ice masses of the poles created opposing apocalyptic swirls, competing, pulling, and torquing the surface plates radiating to the equator with tectonic forces to create mountainous ripples in the liquefying surface which had not yet vaporized. Animate life had already abandoned, and all that remained perished as the world and ninety-eight percent of the atmosphere vanished.

The glaciers of Mare Boreum receded from the northern oceans and from the mountains of the southern hemisphere's Mare Australe. They simply ceased to exist, releasing their ancient ice to be melted and liquified in a momentary torrent or directly sublimated in a more violent outgassing, bypassing the liquid phase in a near instantaneous destruction of what had once been deposited and built up onto the polar mountains over eons of time. The great plains of Arcadia, Arabia and Amenthes emerged from the depths, the waters of which were swept away in a superheated cauldron, while the mountainous regions of Coprates, Tyrrhenum, and Nachos remained broken and buckled under the concussive effects of the accumulating pressures. Both mountains and ocean plains arose, no longer pressed to the surface by the pressure of the waters weight or the disappearing atmosphere. Tectonic plates unseen beneath the surface of the planet undulated and bobbed under the onslaught, and the appearance of what had been solid ground looked like the moving surface of broken ice floes on a swiftly moving torrent. Mountains floated like icebergs on the sea, and the great plains, now exposed from beneath the vanished oceans, split along fault lines as the undulating surface, like plasticized mud, boiled and dried leaving a massively cratered and roughened surface. All moisture and evidence of life succumbed. The shining star that had been the sun in the sky vanished against the logarithmic illumination of the atmosphere, and had already blinded, before it destroyed, any life that had turned in its direction for the last time to sense its warmth and comfort and then lose the source of life and energy in a death so instantaneous that the sensing of its loss itself was lost.

There had been three blue orbs circling round the sun: the second, Venus; the third, Earth; and Mars, the fourth planet. The first of the blue worlds a cauldron of superheated greenhouse gases rich with carbon dioxide and sulfuric clouds which heated the planet to a temperature higher than its distance from the sun would indicate; the second an oasis amidst the other two showing land masses and blue oceans of water capped with ice covered polar regions beneath both dense and wispy rotating clouds; and the third much like the second, with its season generating rotational tilt on its axis, and a similar length of day with mountains, plains, valleys, and oceans beneath its billowy clouds, and surface temperatures nearly identical to the second blue orb's due to the intense greenhouse effect of its richer carbon dioxide atmosphere, in spite of its one-third-again distance from the sun.

Almost two thousand centuries of man and beast and billions of years of oceanic and terrestrial outgassing vanished from the surface and atmosphere as effortlessly from the third blue orb as if there had been a dozen or millions of lost centuries. An extinction event across which its event horizon swallowed all that had been wrought and all that would be lost. A convulsive wave visible from the eighty million kilometers to the second blue planet, a backward horror, historic regret, the tragic inevitability of the sinusoidal peak and trough of life – cold, heat, beast, man, destruction.

The third blue world began to turn red.

The temporal climate was lost, heat and humidity no longer retained in what was left of the exhausted atmosphere. What fraction of carbon dioxide which existed in the previous atmosphere replaced the oxygen molecules consumed through the holocaust, now comprised ninety-five per cent of what remained, and it froze and precipitated out of the air in the polar regions which were blanketed with the rain of dry ice as temperatures reached minus one hundred and fifty degrees

Centigrade in the darkness and frigidity of the nights of Martian sols.

In others parts of the planet, daytime temperatures reached a lifeless twenty degrees Centigrade, but fell far below zero in the cloudless nights. A former shimmering blue like that of the second and third planet, became the remonstrance and the harbinger, the red of decomposing iron and a lost magnetic field, a planet now exposed and unprotected, stripped in the holocaust of its loss.

The atmosphere, consumed and lost in its own destruction was replaced by silence broken only by the periodic winds that were generated by the unmoderated vacillations of modest warmth and bitter cold of day versus nighttime temperatures. Daytime temperature gradients caused the carbon dioxide molecules to move enough to lift dust from the surface, which in turn absorbed heat from the sun. Warming dust clouds moved to cooler areas of the surface, generating wind and lifting more dust and capturing more heat into the air until dissipating in the nights of endless barren sols. In two-thousand centuries, the heated dust, with endless entropic cycles of energy gained and lost, of heat and cold, of atmospheric movement and atmospheric silence, the rising up and the settling down filled the cratered remains in the great plains of Arabia Terra and across the northern latitudes, created shadows thrown against the surface of sterile sand dunes, while dust particles provided a precipitate nucleus to form the carbon dioxide snow which fell in the southern mountains and in the frozen poles.

What had been destroyed and abandoned, cooled through ages of geologic history, and for two hundred thousand years, charged atoms of the remaining atmosphere escaped while the solar wind stripped what was left of atmospheric molecules in a constant passionless, emotionless, uninhabited dissipation. In the planet's postapocalyptic existence, an additional quadrillion kilograms of its thinning atmosphere vanished into the clouds of interplanetary post-solar debris. All that remained was a fine and final dust, and the impact craters buried beneath. Only the protuberant evidence of the Genetic Containment Doors remained, now broken and ajar against the exposed side of Aeolis Mons, the site of the first settlement's broken GCDs, now akimbo, partially destroyed, and swept clean by the scouring effects of wind and dust and sand against the angle of the mountain. The Mons once rose majestically out of a fertile plain which surrounded the caldera lake circling the base of the mountain, all now vanished, the fertile plain and lake now replaced with a barren crater spanning one hundred and fifty kilometers of destruction, silently filled in by the action of the thin, silent, aseptic winds. And the River Paix, the source waters from the mountain, had become an ironic raging torrent of molten silicon dioxide from the mountain sands as it spread out through a breach in the cratering walls like an alluvial fan, cooled, eroded, and in years become ancient, a near diamond-like alluvial surface cloaked in dust.

Were the particle impacts of the solar wind against the surface of the craft amplified a million times, and were the craft listening – as if possible – to hear a beating human heart, the frequency would still be too low as to be perceived by the human mind that constructed it, its voyage now ancient and still silent, the rotation with which it orbits the distant sun is in the cold of near absolute zero. A rumbling imperceptible bass of drumbeats and silent regret, a lifeboat suspended with or without hope of discovery, on an unknown journey to be captured or drowned.

For two hundred millenniums the remaining winds blew across the face of the planet, lifeless dissolution and endless particulate storms, awaiting the return.

II
Quaternary Uinkaret

i

The National System of Interstate and Defense Highways were built in the decades following WWII. This first major postwar construction project in the United States generated much interest and optimism, though also much debate as it crossed and replaced large swaths of cities which were condemned and paved over, and sometimes left to die. Enormous quantities of what was once pristine countryside were consumed for the modern double highways with their sweeping intersections, enabling nonstop long-distance automobile traveling for the first time in the history of the automobile in America. The construction went through, not around, mountains; required the removal of hills and the filling in of valleys, exposing structures and layers of the Earth; the topsoil, subsoils, and the unconsolidated sands, gravels, and clays of the late Quaternary of the Pleistocene Epoch. Lucky children who were taught this geologic history in progressive schools were blessed with science teachers engaged with and open to the modern world of science and technology and the harnessing of the Earth's wonders. Any child might ride their bicycle on an uncompleted highway not yet opened for traffic, and climb the faces of hills excavated through for the roadways and see the layers of the Earth cut open for observation. At a depth measured in years, a child would wonder at the darkened layer of nearly 400,000 years ago with light areas of the Earth above and below, and wonder what had been contained in that which had been buried for the hundreds of thousands of years in which it had lain below the surface, the years which buried the millenniums of achievements and despair of a distant unknown past.

Through the years after our modern world exposed before us with each passing car this signpost of the past, we were allowed brief glances at the scarred surfaces of rolling hills bisected to let a highway through, until the new excavations themselves were overgrown and covered anew. And where the cut was deep enough and the hill high enough, the dark band appeared. If you could only pause from your travels to draw close enough, as the children did that would mountain climb the cuts before the highways opened, and draw closer and closer until your eyes were set against the darkness to allow the light above and below to fall away, you would find yourself in the darkness of a space and time which now existed in only your imagination. With your face pressed against the darkness of the past, you might open up your eyes and see....

ii

The Director – Population Control, stood before the monitor envelopers. Small of stature, but with an authoritative nature, he moved easily about the command structure in which he performed his work. His face was symmetrical, as if drawn by a series of circular shapes that described his features, and most of all the prominence of his slightly protruding gray eyes, illuminated by the screens before him. His compact figure suggested a long-ago athleticism, with an intellect that allowed him to captain teams by the power of his strategic intelligence rather than the limited physical skills he brought to the sports in which he had participated. The brightness of his eyes illuminated his being, the outstanding characteristic evident to all with whom he collaborated.

Humboldt Noraxton, DPC, scanned the monitors that surrounded him. They had moved the entire population from the eastern quadrants of the northern territories, the entire populations of eastern regions across the western seas, and the western regions across the eastern seas, now that the temperatures had begun to moderate. These new holographic monitors with thought control were so much more efficient than the wave touch screen monitors they had been using for the past several decades. Virtual reality, they had theorized, would obviate the need for much of human interaction, but this had been proved wrong; it was useful only as a tool to enhance interaction and communication. It did reduce a significant amount of daily human physical interaction, and though replaced with both sexual and asexual therapy allowances, there were still psychological debates about whether both activities exaggerated a more impersonal emphasis rather than offsetting the negative consequences of the results of virtual reality. It could be argued that the therapies especially, though highly personal and intimate in nature, contributed to a greater distancing of interpersonal interaction. There were unending debates as society had developed in the last millennium. Many adjustments were necessary with the new development of... but the monitors brought him back to work of the day from the musings of his subconsciousness.

"Statistical process control is essential for the monitoring of an advanced technological society. We must discipline ourselves to measure performance, report real time results, and maintain continuous improvement for the well-being of society."

"Furthermore, performance must be measured and reported back, to accelerate the rate of improvement."

The words of Noraxton's Professor of Sociology, Dr. Schraeder Fordcliff, always came back to him as he reviewed the various parameters which appeared before him on the three-dimensional holographic monitors. Fordcliff was the first genius Humboldt had ever personally known. A man who rarely removed the white laboratory coat of a working scientist, whose mature, bloated figure, and sallow complexion belied the athletic prowess he possessed when he was younger. An essential team player, and in later years a towering individual contributing scientist and professor to the highly developed technological society. The kind of man who would memorize a century's worth of statistics on the most arcane of subjects, just for the challenge and fun of it. Who read at least one book a night at the end of each day, and who's seemingly endless energy required half the sleep as that of an average man. His creative application of statistical analysis to the study of human society was a restless achievement, a leap from the measurements of machine to man. More than two hundred years before, during his decades of study and development, these words instilled in Noraxton a basic truth which still resonated with him so many years later. In many ways these simple statements expressed the foundational truth upon which the new society depended.

Data rich, and data dependent we were. It began in understanding the data within the three billion base pairs of DNA which made up each individual's uniqueness, mapped then archived to contain certain determining characteristics of each new child before they began life as a small group of cells, first frozen, and then implanted, to begin a virgin, controlled birth process. Life mimicked math, and still a genetic quantum of variation and determination existed, like the indeterminate location of a single particle in space and time. That the life of each member of society could be measured and analyzed against the DNA database from which they were born, was the legacy of Humboldt's genius professor. But it was not, and never would be possible, to completely remove variation and natural selection from the human genome. It was simply too vast a universe within itself.

Waves of data moved constantly, the reduced summaries of which reached his monitors each moment, immense volumes of data extracted from each element of the new society, whether man or machine, generating millions of petabytes of data points per second. It required first the creation of a virtual mirror image world, and then a reduction of the data to meaningful trends and measurements. Only the most advanced supercomputers, capable of trillions of zettaflops per second, had the capacity to report out these trends of health or maintenance, danger or despair, in support of societal needs and the well-being of man, and of the machines and infrastructure upon which he now depended.

All manner of data needed reporting, and all was reduced to a single reporting node, which floated within upper and lower control limits on the CScale report out screen, available to all citizens in real time reporting, a moving image which changed its prismatic colors depending on trends up or trends down, the higher wavelength colors indicating favorable. But this Comprehensive Scale was in effect a useless measurement, for it could never be permitted to range beneath the lower, the unfavorable control line. What was more important were the various sub-comprehensive markers for items such as births, deaths, diseases, various satisfaction measurements, health statistics, various categories of machine maintenance, production statistics of food and commercial items, water quality, atmospheric composition in the balance of oxygen, nitrogen, and carbon dioxide; of energy production, availability, use, and many more. Of course, Humboldt's responsibilities were for the terrestrial Earth operations alone. There were other streams of data from the interplanetary explorations on the Moon and Mars. Of course, he collaborated with his colleagues on the extraterrestrial reporting, but these were not assigned to his duties, nor were they his daily concerns.

Machine monitoring had come first, developed centuries earlier when the benefits of statistical process control was first understood. The power of the measurement of specific physical parameters, literally to control the deviations of the output of a measurable physical parameter, enabled production management in an entirely new way. Now what was important to understand was not just the count of a machine output, but the measurement of the processes by which the product output was produced. The power of simple math was applied to production management.

For the first time, man applied statistics to understand the processes of the world and not just the literal outputs of a specific action. Eventually we understood that it was how life was controlled and monitored within each living creature, a constant monitoring of the physical processes within each one of us by the redundant and complementing control mechanisms, whether it was the glucose monitoring of blood sugar levels during normal aerobic activity, or the temporary ability of the body under extreme physical distress to perform anaerobic glycolysis, and the subsequent pyruvation of acidic lactate. We began to understand not just how things work, but why they work, and the way in which they do.

Simple control charts were in some ways also comparable to the effective controls embedded within the functions of DNA in the cell nucleus. Messenger RNA takes its instructions from the controlling genetic codes of DNA, to the production sites in the cytoplasm, where amino acids are assembled into proteins – all under the control of the DNA "charts".

More than two hundred years earlier, in the infancy of near-Earth science it was discovered that heavy oxygen marker atoms containing ten neutrons instead of the common eight, could inform us of the Marine Oxygen-Isotope Stages (MIS) of warm and cold climatic changes. Remote sea drilling had provided the ancient deep ocean cores in waters near long abandoned oil drilling platforms. It had been twenty-five thousand years since the present interglacial cycle had begun, and intense frost shattering at unglaciated sites and rising sea levels no longer prevented the movement of the population centers. It had been fifteen thousand years since the rise of the modern species Homo sapiens, and during the previous mass extinction it was theorized that it had not included our genus' ancestors in totality – somehow a branch, though threatened with extinction, had survived and evolved into our present form. Ancient indigenous peoples inhabited parts of the northern and southern continents, as well as the indigenous peoples of the extreme northern polar region – all parts of earlier man which became the foundation for the strength and vitality of our collective species. The 156nd day of year 9,952 had begun well, it was year No. 2 of the 50-year plan that would take humankind's world to the new eleventh millennium. Already there were indications from new deep sea core samples that the next MIS climatic cooling temperature shift would not occur for at least another twenty thousand years.

This meant that there would be a cushion of time to plan for what would eventually be another inevitable K-T, as deadly and merciless as the last near total boundary extinction event caused by an asteroid strike during the Cretaceous Period, a cataclysm marked by the dark iridium containing sediment layer near the Earth's surface, the death sediment which blanketed the world in early geologic time when the Earth's entire terrestrial biosphere burned sixty-five million years ago. The source of the metal iridium found in the sediment blanketing the Earth most assuredly came from meteors and asteroids, where the element exists in much higher concentrations than within the surface of the Earth's crust. During the planet's formation, whatever iridium might have been contained at the surface would have migrated to depths deep below into the Earth, these heaviest elements sinking below the surface. This elemental shiny white death metal is the densest element known to man when space lattice calculations are taken into account. Containing seventy-seven protons and one hundred sixteen neutrons, it is a group nine, d-block, period six transition metal. The evidence of just one of the iridium containing asteroid strikes left a crater one hundred eighty kilometers in diameter, three thousand kilometers to the southeast of the present Uinkaret settlement, yet it was an asteroid with only one-one billionth the mass of the Earth. Many more asteroids fell during that rain of destruction, as the planet passed through a cloud of space debris that caused the world to burn – perhaps as many as hundreds or thousands of asteroids burst though the skies in a prolonged and deadly strike, caused time to stand still for thousands and millions of years, and in the cataclysmic cleansing would enable the rise of mammals and eventually the rise of man.

Less than one hundred years after the first Earth launched satellites achieved escape velocity and began to orbit the Earth at an astonishing eight kilometers per second, the space above the Earth began to be overpopulated with satellites, as each of the world's developing population centers rushed to launch their own satellites. These centers celebrated their mastery of this obsolete and inefficient technology, and soon low-Earth-orbit space debris cluttered the super-stratospheric fields above the surface of the Earth. Space defense activity of the various centers which still existed at that time experimented with destructor satellites with the hope that this technology would protect against meteors and asteroids large enough to damage or destroy the Earth's environment, using physical, explosive, and wave-based detonations to deter and destroy threatening objects in space. Eventually the triggering of ill-thought-out experimental destructions filled the low Earth orbital lanes with countless pieces of space debris speeding at 29,000 kilometers per hour. Eventually, all of the satellites were allowed to fall from orbit, as their functions were replaced by a new, quantum, nuclear based technology. Massive particle detection devices had allowed the discovery of new subatomic particles, and neutrino wave physics of sub-particle nuclear structures were theorized and developed – antistructures and antimatters were proposed, refuted, proposed again and then validated. Physical presence and physical borders eventually fell away as the world's wealth and political structures consolidated, and the need for space-based satellites was obsoleted.

So it was that in the ensuing century, after stationary and orbiting Earth satellites were permitted to fall, virtual neutrino wave sensors were deployed to provide superior performance without the need of orbiting satellites to replenish thruster fuel or penetrate atmospheric interference. These advanced virtual holographic devices, powered by neutrino/anti-neutrino lasers beamed from Earth, were fully deployable at any longitude, latitude, or altitude, capable of almost instantaneous redirection within a 45-degree arc of view. Two thousand virtual sensors were deployed, each monitoring approximately two hundred fifty thousand square kilometers, providing full coverage for the protective monitoring of the entire planet from any space-based danger, or terrestrially launched threat.

Still, ongoing research hinted at a potential fourth dimensional nano-gargantuan event horizon. Gravity, the weakest known force in the universe, led us to search for the strongest forces, and the terrible knowledge of those forces. Man could now take action to delay, dispel, or prevent another K-T event sourced from the heavens. Terrestrial war, man versus man, had been outlawed and abandoned for more than a thousand years, a natural evolution and positive correlation to the length of lifespan increase. For hundreds of years though in the past millennium, the depth of the seas was still more distant than the nearest planets and the moon. Now the seas had also been mapped and understood, but what remained deep inside the Earth remained as unknown as the distant stars whose light could at least be split and analyzed with spectrographic analysis. It was the unknown from the unknown depths of the Earth from which both fortune and tragedy could arise, the reward or risk of life or death.

The Union of United Countries Confederation had long since been made obsolete and replaced by the Inter-Planetary Confederation, what with the permanent outposts now settled on Mars. The old subterranean rare lunar metals mining operations on the moon were exhausted after six decades, and with the discovery of synthetic substitutes for elemental necessities, new expansions to the challenging subterranean lunar operations were no longer required. Since the succeeding generation had not experienced the need for lunar moon metals, and with no alternative commercial demand, interlunar travel was no longer as attractive, nor interesting enough to continue regular tourist excursions, which had been in effect subsidized by the mining operations. The interest of the younger generation had moved on to Mars. The moon was now merely an interplanetary slingshot, interesting enough only from the closest flyby that was possible using the gravity enhanced orbital boost for the journey to the fourth planet. We are an interplanetary species now, thought Humboldt, and the I-P

Confederation had proudly recognized this fact when the Mars colony was granted its charter in perpetuity.

Problems, problems, problems, thought Humboldt. There is no end to the problems of planning and organizing the implementation of plans. Since the dawn of biogenetics, both disease and behavior had largely been metastasized to a benign state. A hyperplastic growth of knowledge exploded after a long gestation spanning the last millennium, so that by the end of the previous millennium – year 9,000 – to the near turn of the present, the fate and the characteristics of man had changed. The challenge was to retain the essential, and to eradicate the morbid. Mankind no longer needed fear disease and chronic illness. Suffering was no longer rampant nor considered the inevitable fate of man. Hunger of the peoples in the Confederation was nonexistent. and those excepted from the new settlements by force of will, stubbornness, or the false equivalence of solitary freedom would not survive, or would survive only by the presence of the Uinkaret at the margins. The first non-avian beasts of nature, those creatures of land and sea – none of these had survived the K-T extinction eons earlier. The new non-avian species, were life not descended from the gigantic animals of the ancient past. They had descended and lived and thrived in the interglacial periods. The Councils knew that this current period would also one day end, though far enough into the future for its planned transition and the survival of man, flora, and fauna. That is, the chosen flora and fauna that would survive with the chosen man. There were signs, but it was thought that there would be sufficient time to prepare.

But there were problems which continued unabated, problems and challenges to be addressed and resolved. The greatest discovery of biogenetic science had found the gene series responsible for length of life; the clock that commanded cells to begin to age and to atrophy, and eventually cease to function in a cascading failure resulting in man's morbidity and death. This was known to be a necessary part of natural selection, a speeding up of the cycle of life and death and the survival and success of the fittest to carry on. It had not been understood what effect this genetic length of life discovery would have on society – in the beginning for the privileged few only – and what the eventual result would be for a nominally aged population. The wars, famines, and the rise of new lethal variant viruses of the Ninth Millennium had reduced the global population by eighty per cent, so that only four million had remained. Understanding the lifespan gene at position 4q75.3 on the minus strand of chromosome IV would eventually enable an increase to the life span of the population by a minimum five hundred percent of previous generations. This was not sustainable with the current position of the receding glaciers and sea level rise. The technology required to perform a single-nucleotide polymorphism on an SNP locus of the 4q gene was eventually developed. And it was understood that the resultant rise in population would have to be controlled by limiting fertility rates. It was also decided that such humans would have to be centralized to a protected area – each succeeding decade and century of a successful and contributing life would increase the value to the community of the genetically boosted individual. Previously inhabited areas now vacated were returned to the wild, and species of animals and fauna flourished. It presented an interesting anomaly, in that a protected, lengthened human life span would be surrounded by a greater natural world of plants and animals. An irregularity of man reduced to a controlled environment, versus a normality of nature which expanded the natural and wild world.

The order of lengthening had to be decided. It made sense to start at the top of society's pyramid and work to the bottom, with the exception that if an individual was deemed essential at any social strata, that person was moved up two orders of social importance when they received the right to have their genetic alteration, and begin her or his lengthened lifespan. There had been of course discussions on the excision or inclusion of the sexuality behavioral genetic markers, which of course for decades and generations had no longer been necessary for the procreation of the species. But this proposal was, interestingly enough, defeated by females who feared that those identified as males might no longer be interested in sexual behavior. The female population felt a potential loss of future control with the takeover and obviation of the male versus female identities. It was an interesting fact of the history of man that the male of the species was willing to give up sexuality as a method of procreation in exchange for greater power and independence. It was the women who objected, who still wanted marriage rituals, and the practices and co-dependencies which allowed them the ability to use sexual control. Of course, this had led to the eventual total equality of the sexes, and sexual therapy allowance urge control.

The general order and function of the human chromosomes had long been understood, an order similar to the stages of the development of the brain, from the basic physical functions of the 1st Tertiary chromosomes, the "brain stem" if you will, to the chromosomes of the higher and deeper functions of the 2rd and 3rd Tertiaries, along with the consciousness developed in the 22nd chromosome pair, to finally the sexuality traits of the 23rd. With the discovery of the single-nucleotide polymorphism locus on chromosome IV of the 1st Tertiary, which effects end of life function and diseases, the lifespan of man in a theoretical projection could approach even a millennium of years. Perhaps a life everlasting was even possible could a haven be constructed where man could live in a protected environment with the technology to monitor unending genetic life.

Still, it was humbling to consider the human chromosomes compared to the first mapped genome, that of the common fruit fly, the Drosophila melanogaster. We had considered ourselves to be infinitely more complex than the mere swat of a fruit fly, but in truth we discovered that our DNA protein interactions were merely ten times that of the fruit fly, and a mere twenty times that of a single cell yeast! Eventually we learned that not just the quantity but also the complexity of protein interactions determined the biological complexity of an organism. One trait in particular bears comparison to that of the fruit fly. In we humans, spatial visual processing – that is, the resolution of our eyesight – is much superior to the humble fly. But as anyone knows who has tried to swat one away, the fruit fly's temporal resolution – that is, the refresh rate of its sight – is ten times faster than ours. It is much superior in small spaces to evade our irritated movements to try to destroy the offending insect. Most astounding of all – and not meeting our previous expectation – it was discovered that most of the genes of the Drosophila melanogaster are conserved or represented by homologous genes in humans responsible for many of the same basic life processes – the mapping of the complexity of a body structure complete with a central nervous system, the designs of the homeotic or master genes that determine the development of all body parts – the stem cell holy grail. The keys with which to open the locks of the universe of life, the building blocks and function of DNA, was a key scientific discovery.

Eventually during the middle years of the tenth millennium it was agreed that all humans were to repatriate to the Uinkaret Prefecture, a haven place untouched by the most recent glaciation cycles of the last geologic period. A place noted world-wide for its fine climate and natural beauty, and where procreation could be managed for the new centuries of man. A population diminished in number but controlled, managed, perfected, and protected, whose lifespans so increased that at any time the number of productive adult man-years lived by the current Earth's living members would equal that which the Earth could sustain were the number of living individuals twenty times as great.

Humboldt's four-hour morning workday was coming to an end. He was still not accustomed to the longer work hours, nor was he convinced of the need. Workdays had increased thirty-three per cent since the unification decree had been issued in year one of the Fifty-Year Plan. Three hours of work per day had been sufficient in order to provide for basic needs, but not for the sufficient stimulations and stress to maintain healthy mental capabilities. The three-hour day became the four-hour day.

"Our lives might have been lengthened," thought Humboldt as he descended to the level of the concourse on the gravity equalizer platform, with the barely discernable sound of the spinning centrifuges within its works, "but our work is more exhausting, and the longer hours more punishing. Try to see if you can manage the monitor envelopers, and maintain your effectiveness over a new-to-human modern work schedule," he complained to himself.

He remembered that the theory said the increased hours and modest stress were important for long term physical and mental health. At the same time, STAs, Sexual Therapy Allowances, were increased to a daily quota, from only five per week, with carryover allowed of up to five visits per month, to be taken by the end of each succeeding month. Especially difficult days were assuaged by multiple visits if one were able to plan ahead, and the monthly expiration encouraged the healthy inducement to use or lose this health enhancing entitlement. Between sexually linked individuals, sex chits could be exchanged, and it was an interesting statistic that there was a greater borrowed sexual frequency by the female population. It was said that private activity which was still lawful, was deemed more desirable by the male populace. Females voluntarily exchanged this private activity for the preference of a greater frequency of the more clinical, less personal interactions provided within the safety and anonymity of Club facilities provided by society.

Before attending to the Club, as they referred to these facilities, Humboldt had to choose between the bicycle or the car, both self-riding or self-driving as an option, or manual control by the rider as in ancient times alone, and he chose to bicycle along the river in manual control as it worked its way through the shallow canyons. It was a lovely day, the sun was still near the zenith in the sky, just beginning to cast his moving shadow northward on the south rim of the guideway as he sat atop his self-balancing machine with its tiniest whisper of solid-state gyros. Artificially noise was automatically generated at the approach for the benefit of proximate individuals who otherwise may not be aware of the silently moving objects. In the distance, balanced against the nature forest, the glint of the sun reflected off the banks of glass of the city buildings in the metallic dichroic colors of these transparent panels – the result of the chemical vapor deposition manufacturing process which produced them – reflecting an artificially altered palette against the leaves of trees, the nature within which its architecture had been placed, as if it too was produced in an artificial vacuum.

A few steps from the glidepath found him on the valley floor, and at the entrance to the STA Club. He enjoyed this daily routine, though the morning's work was exhausting. Mieke and Ekta greeted him as he entered, his presence detected from the tiny spec of gallium arsenide embedded below his left wrist as he approached.

No two individuals of opposite sex could be more desirable and yet more unalike. Statistically average in height, at 168 and 185 centimeters, was their only commonality – from there, their attributes both physical and emotional diverged.

Ekta, raven-haired, presented himself with no pretense of gentleness. He wore his hair pulled back severely from his face, away from the crown of his head and temples. He wore tiny unadorned gold loop earrings. The only hint of gentleness in his visage being the child-like wisps of hair at his temples, not long enough to be swept back with the rest of his coarse curls which would fall to his shoulders, were they not gathered together into a tight top knot. Dark eyes, a straight nose, and lips not thin, but only half full, like his smile. His body was totally symmetrical in proportions, his head one-seventh the height of his body, with shoulders, waist, and length of legs, all normal for his height and obvious strength and athleticism beneath his loose, form-fitting clothing. Business-like, almost aggressive in his civil greetings, merely a disguise of his over-riding social shyness which went unabated until his therapies began. Then a release only in private, overpowering and physically emotional with his clients.

Mieke was as physically demonstrative as were her emotions, displayed openly. It was the natural inclination in which she interacted with clients, friends, or strangers. Hair the color of heather, short and bobbed about her face, it reached only to the nape of her neck, just covering her ears which held simple platinum studs. Her face was more rounded and her features softer, with laughing eyes – blue or green depending on the light or the angle – as bright as her smile which radiated from her visage. A femininity as well-proportioned overall as Ekta's masculine strength, but with a small bust, a shorter waist, and longer slender legs. She was a natural dancer, comfortable in social or private relations. As uninhibited at the first greeting with her clients, as privately when her therapies began.

Only those few clients who preferred a voyeuristic pleasure, perceived a union between the two of them which was as intense as an uncontrolled exothermic chemical reaction.

"Hello, Dr. Noraxton," they greeted him, as he entered, and he smiled at these two most perfectly formed human beings. He could feel the stress escaping with the anticipated pleasure and the small imperceptible shudder within his already relaxing core as he prepared to cast off all social restraint. Within the next sixty minutes of his allotted hour, he would rid himself of the rest of his stress, then ascend to the glide path on the rim, and return to his flat to change clothes and enjoy the afternoon and evening amidst the shops and cafes and entertainment of the Uinkaret Social Containment Complex, where other more involved pleasures might take place.

iii

There was no shortage of power in the modern world. Scientific advancement had long conquered the problem of energy generation, storage, and distribution. Electricity had become the distributed power of choice, the problem and untidiness of tethers to physical cables had long since been solved. The classical subatomic particle theories gave rise to the understanding of quantum and wave-based reality which combined   strange   particle   behaviors   with   multiple simultaneous positions of indeterminate matter theories. This could only be explained by the existence of energy waves, not long after the ancient discovery of gravitational waves which had required enormously precise structures – though crude by modern standards – built by the ancients. Combining these theories, along with theories of power generation fusion control, was a process that took longer than the previous century of scientific discovery, but it led to a newly energized world, and a world order of limitless, wireless, electrical energy distribution, and the highly technical devices capable of receiving the untethered energy. Still, this new resource required the implementation of strict controls, without which chaos had briefly ensued, when this energy infrastructure was first installed and the extent of frivolous and wasteful uses caused widespread energy outages.

There were still natural processes to monitor in the Uinkaret, and it was not so much control or containment as it was a symbiotic concession to nature. There would always be powers of nature greater than those that man could control. This understanding had for centuries been resisted by the political parties of the past. In some ways it was no different than the evolution and adaptation between the sexes, whereas woman and man no longer coupled only in the ways of the old societies. The concepts of marriage and procreation, and even the identities of sexual traits had long since been understood, if not abandoned outright – society had long ago begun to travel an asymptote toward a final understanding between the sexes. Love still existed, but all who allowed that emotion became long distant travelers, now that lives were measured in centuries, not decades. Love became both broader and deeper, but most experienced it with a frequency renewal now spread over centuries, allowing time itself to produce a kind of reincarnation.

So too, man's relationship to nature advanced to a more sustainable level with a longer-term perspective lengthened to the extent of a human's longer life. Now a lifespan was long enough to perceive and experience environmental changes which in the past were only affected across generations. This new perspective imposed a new longer-term sense of responsibility and stewardship. Scientific advances had enabled an understanding and documentation of climactic changes that occurred since the beginning of the solar system, more than four and a half billion years to the present, and it was understood that the interglacial period in which we now lived was a frequency cycle beyond man's control. The Interplanetary Space Debris Doomsday Project had informed us of the cataclysmic extinction events that were epochal possibilities coming from space. We were surrounded by a statistic of danger, yet we were a survival species, and now that we had progressed to the point in which we found ourselves, our survival became of greater and greater value. We understood that we could not afford to lose everything to an entropy of natural or man-made destruction. Too much was now understood, there were resources never before available to humankind with our understanding of this world and our place within the solar system and the universe. There was still the instinct to survive with the difference being that now we, for the first time in human history, were a race of women and men who wielded the tools of their own survival.

As Humboldt entered his flat, he asked that a coffee be prepared. The crude voice recognition technology first developed in the previous century now made life so much easier, seamlessly integrated into the simple tasks of living. Putting away his morning cup from the food preparation counter where he had left it in the morning, he took a fresh cup from the cupboard and placed it in the machine which ejected the spent capsules and inserted a new one as he spoke to the machine to describe the kind of coffee he wanted to drink. Some of his friends had installed machines that provided total automation, but Humboldt still enjoyed a minimal participation in the coffee ritual, as much as some of his more formally inclined colleagues continued to practice traditional tea rituals. This desire for, this need for the ritual of a preparation, was something still retained deep in the human psyche. At his age he no longer found it necessary to partake of the nitrogen containing organics – the isoquinoline heterocyclic aromatics, phenanthrenes, and phenethylamine herbal varieties which had been proven too maliciously and dependently causal if used in the first two hundred years of life. He opened the door to the balcony and exited the room, coffee in hand. Coffee, it turned out, became his most essential drug of choice.

The optimum RFSP – the Rotational Frequency for Spousal Partners – was determined to be between thirty to sixty years, though individuals were allowed to retain preferential adjustments on the timing of their movements. But it was certainly unusual for an RFSP of less than twenty years, or more than eighty, and it was usually a decision that needed to be imposed on an individual by societal rules since in the manner of human tendencies, most people were still change adverse to what would have been possible in an entire lifetime of companionship prior to the discovery of the lifespan gene, and in the absence of a moving decree, many would remain where they were, with whom they were with, and in this significant way lose the vitality of life. Of course, in cases of extreme prejudice an immediate marriage annulment was still possible and preferred to the alternative of a disastrous spousal union. It was simply another well-founded finding that without a twenty or thirty-year generational turnover which had been the human condition for thousands of years, there was still a need for change – no one could imagine a colleague or neighbor unchanged for a hundred years or more. We had become more sophisticated but we did not want to become increasingly bored. Such a dramatic increase in one's life span forced changes that still seemed generationally bound. In fact, it was much simpler than that. As the sexual therapy need was discovered, so too was the development of Social Turnover Interaction Ratios, now a departmental organization, STIR, within the Confederation's Population Management Division managed by Humboldt, and which reported to his LifeWatch Directorate. It was this Directorate that determined the optimum RFSP.

It was difficult for Humboldt to remove his professional life from his personal life. In the day already more than half spent, he had exited his work space, visited the Club, returned refreshed from the bicycle enjoyment and sexual fulfillment, changed clothes, made another coffee, and stood sipping it calmly as he surveyed the spectacle around him. Dimmed and undimmed glass enclosures faced him, enclosing individuals and couples in various degrees of modesty or exhibitionism. But there was always the nagging fear, the possibility of change, of unsustainable effort, of relentless entropy. With a wave of his hand, he brought up the broad outlines of his responsibilities on a holographic display, and stood, considering the image in front of him.

Reporting to the Interplanetary Confederation- Earth

Director, Population Control
Humboldt Noraxton b. 9619
Status – unmatched – age 333 years

Sub-Directorships
- BreedLove, registration for guardians and fertilization
- LifeWatch, healthcare
- PalmCare, the victory of a complete life
- PrimRein, protection of mutation research

Something was missing, although he had been part of this organization going on nearly twenty-six decades since the end of the ninety-seventh century when he was appointed at age seventy-three as an analyst reporting to the previous Population Control Director. The preceding Fifty-Year Plan had been moderately successful. LifeWatch had had to deal with no major disease outbreaks, genetic boosting had replaced virus control due to the research conducted by PrimRein, and the wisdom of the organization's synergies had proven themselves.

He had insisted on that conflation himself, even though he had only been assigned as Director- PC for less than forty years, and was only two hundred ninety-five years old when he had assumed responsibility. Less than twenty years earlier he had been assigned to manage the fourth sub-directorship of Population Control – PrimRein.

Humboldt's Club activities had proved as satisfying as his previous spousal assignments, perhaps at times even more, but still there was the nagging doubt. Something far in the future, something beyond the settlements in Mars, perhaps beyond the dwarf planet Makemake and the Kuiper belt which was only now beginning to be explored. Perhaps it was much closer to home, perhaps it was deep below the surface of the Earth, and the hope that it was far into the future.

Humboldt Noraxton had already enjoyed four spousal assignments, and was taking a few decades off before being assigned to a requested fifth. Perhaps in another hundred years he would consider the possibility of a child. A Matchmake Gametogenesis Application could wait for now, there was no need to rush the MGA. At age three hundred thirty-three he had already been espoused for a total of one hundred ninety-five years. He had found his first spousal assignment at the age of forty-five to be the most satisfying. It was an experience that was quite the usual, and most found that the completion of the first assignment was the most difficult to do. The special first, and then the first letting go. In each subsequent relationship most couples found it easier to transition and move on with their lives, as there began the realization that there was yet much to experience, enjoy, and contribute to society. The richness of multiple relationship experiences compensated for the natural instinct of the reluctance to let go of relationships pleasant and compatible.

That was of course a testament to the success of the RFSP and STIR research and the Genetic Pre-dispositional Couples Match, all administered by PalmCare. The function of PalmCare's Life Victory Counseling was also to separate, sooth, educate, and encourage the former spousal partners to make a healthy break with the past, and to look forward to the future. Humboldt was a normal healthy citizen in this respect, and espoused again at age 125, 200, and for the fourth time at age 290. His experiences were satisfying and with a fifth future spousal partner he intended to have a companion with whom they would conceive their first child. Of course, it would be a perfectly engineered conception, but still a conception which required contractual responsibilities to a child from both parents, a responsibility which would last for hundreds of years and through multiple layers of spousal relationships, an unstitched thread that ran through lengthened lives.

iv

Humboldt entered the Social Containment Complex from the glidepath which had taken him from the building in which his flat was located into the heart of the four million resident city. The Plex, as it was called, was the heart of the city, but this area in which the world's most advanced humans now resided was more than just the population center. Within its area had been consolidated all of the makings of a human haven into which all production, both material and biogenetic, was funneled, in order to sustain the fewer, longer lived, more advanced, more efficient humans of this modern world in this singular place. The Plex enabled the after-hours benefits for all the achievements of its inhabitants. It was an ever-changing assortment of offerings by which to entertain and enrich the lives of these chosen people, all of whom had a synergistic part in the social fabric which had clothed its people for centuries now, not decades. It was the heart of the Uinkaret Prefecture, the great city, the chosen place, the place designed by the foremothers and fathers of the new human order.

Decades had become centuries. The development of technological capability and the lifespan extension meant that memory and past experiences multiplied, and with it the effect of speeding up change in a counterintuitive way. Each person's personal history extended backwards to centuries, and now included what would have been a span of several generations and lifetimes. The time needed to process these now lengthy lifetimes meant that there was much to consider and time needed to consider it. Yet the capacity of the human brain was easily capable of a millennium's worth of information for emotion, memory, function, performance, and the desire for historically endless work and play – the biological desire for life itself of a conscious being. It was as if the human mind and body, freed from genetic decay, had no limit in its passion to exist. With the benefit of an individual's experience and knowledge gained in a contiguous lifetime of adult thought, it was now unbroken from what before had taken generations of adult only thought, available only between the early years of birth and development, and the final years of frailty and death. Knowledge and understanding were now able to progress in an individual's lifespan in a perennially uninterrupted stream of centuries.

Pure water flowed from the mountains to the north, source waters for the life blood of the desert city. Heat during the day, and the coolness of the evenings were controlled with the expenditure of little energy, even though low-cost energy generation was now almost limitless. Entire double-roof structures of buildings were raised to vent the heat of midday summers, with subterranean openings drawing cooler air below ground to circulate through the structure and exhaust through the open inner roof. During the nights of winter months, passively stored solar heat was released into the subterranean chambers and radiated through the buildings with an opposite effect. Enough water pressure was generated from the waters flowing south to reach to the fifth floors above ground, with the need to provide water pressure only to buildings that rose above that height. Intense pinpricks of powerful light sources illuminated rooms in all manner of style and comfort, moderated by fixtures energized by wireless electrical transmissions from the chemical, electronic, and nuclear based miniature lumen generators. By and large there was sound control in public places, the sounds of daily commerce strictly limited to hours and places and volume. There was no longer public place encroachment of music or broadcast messages. If a citizen desired certain sounds, or entertainment, news, or music, it was incumbent upon himself to provide it for his own personal enjoyment without imposing unwanted sounds to distract those around him. There were no personal vehicles permitted within a certain distance from the center of the city. Public transportation was available everywhere in the city, never with more than a few minutes wait, and personal fare transportation, though also strictly regulated, was available to anyone everywhere for those who had a special need or timely requirement. It had taken a thousand years of technology to create all these things and then to make them part of the unobtrusive nature of the city, accommodating to residents exhibiting voluntary self-restraint –not needing to bend the will of the residents to societal planning. The excess of possessions and consumer goods which had created such a calamitous effect in the primitive and short-lived centuries past in the years before man learned to use what he wanted and needed, and not be controlled by the goods around him, eventually taught him to recognize and abrogate the possibilities for destructive and unhealthy forms of comfort in the postmodern world. It was even as if preventing an unwanted biological function. These had been the results of an uncontrolled consumer society which was much more successful in fulfilling man's more immediate base desires, instead of those more sustainable to benefit future generations.

Having lost himself in thought along the way, Humboldt now entered the Flaxen Café, with its alternating blue and yellow walls, and was waved to a table where three of his oldest friends were already seated.

Alfrieda Praxis, Professor of Environmental Science
at Teknikobstant University

Konstantina Oblation, Esquire, Office of Legal Ownership

Rotfach Theoretrics, Managing Director, Rundfunk Kt.

Rundfunk was originally founded as a manufacturer of technical measurement devices used for both organic and inorganic applications, an historically important company whose history included groundbreaking DNA decoding accomplished a thousand years prior under the auspices of the original founder of the company, Professor Marcus Funk. The founding professor had developed nano-microwave detection measurement devices using a wholly innovative process compared to the older technology of electron microscopic technology which did not have the capability to resolve molecular shapes and structures of chemical compositions necessary for gene splicing biogenetics. Over the centuries it had become a consortium of companies capable of designing and building entire cities and city infrastructure in ways that nearly mimicked natures genetic processes.

Humboldt sat with the friends he had known since university days, or in the several decades after he had begun his career. Rotfach and Alfrieda since his student days, and Konstantina who had become a colleague with overlapping issues of population control affecting real and personal property. Initially unforeseen ownership issues had evolved along with the increasing lifespans. Certain legalities were now many times more complicated with length of life issues. These could now span multiple centuries. Spousal unions and the births of children now occurred decades or centuries apart with different partners. Special legal considerations were required to accommodate what would have been successive generations in the previous millennium. Now these more complex legal instruments needed to be constructed to protect what were now merely different phases of a single life span.

Rotfach Theoretrics sat poised with the tension of an alloy spring under pressure. Deep set eyes peered out from his protruding brow of a surviving gene-set, a ruddy complexion half shadowed by his unkempt mane and rough, sparse beard which belied the completeness of his intellect. He was not a tall man, but the former athleticism of his figure – all citizens were required in their youth to participate in sports – was not completely hidden by his slightly rumpled appearance. Though the tailoring of his clothing was impeccable, he just did not consider the importance of his appearance, and he wore his entire visage with an unconcerned carelessness. But his excited anticipation could not be concealed. He was eager to begin the evening with his friends. He loved their debating banter, and he did so with an impassioned emotion.

"Norax, you look worried, my friend," intoned Rotfach.

"What is on your mind that concerns you so late in this day?" he continued.

"You need to learn to let things go and enjoy what you have earned. Days are long when you do not use all of your allotted STAs. Have you been taking care of yourself?" he tapped his wrist where the gallium arsenide chip was embedded.

"I'm afraid that you are wrong on that score," Humboldt replied, with the pleasant thought of Ekta and Mieke at the reception in the Club earlier in the afternoon, and the STA session with one of the talented therapists.

"I'm very glad to hear it, my friend."

"The first three hundred years of your life have not been bad, and I say that you've got at least four hundred yet to enjoy, and perhaps double that!"

Rotfach waved his hand over the table's sensor to order his friend a drink.

"I wager that you'll last a millennium. I'll buy the first round, young man, but your chip is going to pay for the next," said Rotfach, raising a glass to his lips.

Rotfach was his oldest friend, Humboldt took his seat, and responded.

"I'll take this drink, and raise you," and he nodded to the others at the table.

As usual, the debate had already begun. It did not take all four of them for the discussions to begin, any two of them with passionate effect would readily open an argument; any two of them together was enough to begin a debate. So intense were their discussions, that for a period of ten years at one point, the businessman would not speak to the professor. But all was eventually forgiven, and friends they were for centuries past and friends they would remain for centuries to come, science and the environment, willing. Rotfach, the only entrepreneur at the table, was bellicose and bombastic.

"Let the bureaucrats bureaucratize!" he cried.

It took three of the others, the two fonctionnaires and the professor, to balance out Rotfach's irrepressible energy against which logic was no match. A salient mix of venerated individuals, love more constant than with changeable spousal partners, not only by virtue of the age of their friendship, but by the energy and passion with which they approached their lives and worked at their varied professions in concert for the betterment of the modern society in which they lived.

"Surely more than one of us needs to stimulate the economy and pay for the rest of our sins!" Rotfach laughed, a well-placed dig he liked to use as frequently as possible.

"Can I be the only income producing member of our group? Is it justice that one provides the economic production for four? I feel I am overtaxed literally and figuratively when I am in your midst!"

Perhaps one example of the source of a ten-year feud within their group.

"Humboldt," said Rotfach, "is it true that you will have a child with your next companion?" changing the subject now that he had made his point.

Humboldt was the childless one among them.

"How many years is it since you did not live alone?" he added.

"It has been more than thirty years since my last spousal assignment," replied Humboldt, "and at my age of three hundred plus years, I have used up only one third of my life if I can believe the lifespan you attribute to me. I have finally begun to have the feeling and the desire that I want to have a child after all these years, though I never felt the desire at any time between myself and the women of my first four spousal engagements. There was always so much to do and to enjoy, and to be selfish with our possibilities, and perhaps because we were still so young, and knowing that spousal assignments were temporary and there was always the looking forward to the next one. That it was something to be enjoyed again after a period of being alone and knowing that solitude would not be permanent. That a new spouse was always available. That there was a lot of security in knowing that there would be both periods of companionship and solitude in life, but never an aloneness. That there was never a permanent solitude of one. I feel different now that I am older and more experienced, and am no longer concerned about the temporary nature of a spousal assignment. Nor am I doubtful that I am able to give a child the full measure of my love."

"What we have now is something the ancients could not attain with their brief lives and tenuous relationships," added the lawyer Konstantina, unemotional, cool and composed, unflappable in public. She was a tall sophisticated woman, dark hair and fair complexion, piercing ocean eyes, a beauty with an intellect that shone through, commanding respect.

She continued, "For them there was only one real chance of an extended relationship and life was over in far less than a century of years. As often as not, what they called a marriage failed with the result that for many of the ancient elders only mere brief multiple marriages were possible. Worse was when a marriage failed and a socially limiting aloneness followed. It is fortunate that we suffered that quaint custom for only a few millenniums. Our new ways seem more natural and truer to me now, and so much more human than the highly restricted brevity of the marriages of ancient history."

"My son is already one hundred fifty years old," said Alfrieda, "from my second assignment and spousal companion Compurtna. I was only one hundred seventy-three years old but we both felt the need and desire for a child, and wanted a longer life together with our first child than most assignments provide for. I do not regret it, and though I have only had three assignments- the third was not as fulfilling as the second with our child, but soon I will request a fourth spousal assignment and perhaps consider another second child, if the assignment is passionate enough – and desirous enough, that is."

"But I wanted to talk about another subject today," Alfrieda continued, a smaller woman with a compact figure, prone to allowing her emotions to run free among friends, or when discussing the passion of her life, the environment.

"It has been, what? How many years?" she thought out loud again, "since our virtual world began replacing the physical?"

"Here we go again, Frieda," interjected Konstantina, "always the environmental consideration, the professorial breakthrough with indignant urgency. Do you have imagination for anything else?"

"Wait a moment, please allow me to explain," tried Alfrieda, but Rotfach also interrupted her for the second time.

"It's OK, Frieda. Konstantina does not have an emotional bone in her body. You're an entirely cold-blooded lawyer, Konstance, and if we still used books, yours would all be dry and dusty. But don't take it personally," he laughed at his friend, "I still love you," said Rotfach, the entrepreneur, who still needed both passion and ruthless control to be successful in his profession.

"But seriously," Alfrieda began again, "that's the point. Do any of us still imagine that we miss the things that the ancients had to use? They did have actual books to read and to hold, like the ones displayed now only in the library archives of museums. Nobody has really used them now for generations and generations. Only if given as a gift or as a curiosity as a remembrance of the ancients and how far we have come in the history of humankind."

"We leave nothing behind but digital renderings of our existence, all so accessible in searchable databases of our lives. But imagine the world outside of the Uinkaret if you were unable to transport the technology with you," Alfrieda continued.

"Please do not misunderstand me, I have no desire to live in a world without our technological comforts and conveniences," she added.

"I would never want to go back to the ancient times, but still, when our lives are over, our existence is as erasable as a digital record floating in a quantum sea of uncertainty," concluded Rotfach.

"It is true," said Humboldt, "that what we now leave behind is dependent on the accessible technology to support it in our digital archives, but there is no going back. Imagine the almost infinite weight of a physical documentation system."

"I wonder sometimes," concluded Alfrieda Praxis, the professor of environmental science, "about the Confederation's decisions in the last mid-millennium to digitize, then dismantle and remove the ancient physical infrastructures of data, documents, and images, and the argument being that it was necessary to prevent the continuance of a shadow society opposed to the progress we have made here in the Quaternary."

"It was the right decision," said Rotfach, without the slightest hint of the advantage that accrued to his company which profited greatly from both the building up of the Quaternary Uinkaret, and the dismantling of the old infrastructures, the roads and bridges, satellite monitoring stations, oil platforms, power plants, energy grids, and water control structures, and the obviated ancient's cities themselves.

In five hundred years since the DOE, the Decree of the Erasing, when the great dismantling had begun, the Confederation moved to consolidate control over human society justified by the successful lengthening of human life, and the explosion of data required to infrastructure a society which required a more technological life. Nature responded and covered, overgrew, and erased from visible sight what was left after the destruction and removal of almost all human settlement sites which had taken non-digital man thousands of years to discover, and to build, and to write about.

"Drinks, ladies and gentlemen, drinks!" cried Rotfach.

He and Konstantina raised and brought their glasses together, then turned to meet the others as they raised their glasses as well.

"Humboldt is buying more drinks!" he said, taking Humboldt's wrist and moving it over the censor. Now the four evening companions, one for each of the friends, came to sit with them, turning to the music, the drinks, and the evening of entertainment, including the optional sexual dreamscapes which would follow.

v

The Flaxen Café fell away to the recesses of his consciousness as his companion took the drink from his hand. It was a kind of cocktail of fermented fruit which bore the taste of apricots, peaches, grapes, mangoes, and pomegranates, a distillation of ripened fruit and pure mountain water, and suddenly it seemed to Humboldt that they exited an altered café from which they had been shoulder to shoulder with the patrons crowding the bar, and he knew only that it was not the Flaxen. It was a place to drink, and dance, and to let go your inhibitions as you allowed the music and the cocktail to take over your emotions. A solitary dancer moved, eyes closed, rhythmically swaying to the music, in front of the band, oblivious to the crush of people around him, lost in the ancient music they were playing that evening and absorbed in his own solitary meditation in a dreamlike slow-motion movement. Someone standing next to Humboldt asked him if he knew the name of the song they played, but his mind could not focus and he could not recall, and the stranger turned to ask his question of another. They ascended the ancient stone steps, slabs of granite which led to the street above the level of the subterranean gathering place for music, drinks, comradery, and the election of partners for the hours to come. They walked through cobbled streets and ancient buildings, as if in a dream from the distant past and continued on through the city streets, resembling a village reconstructed, with shops, and cafés, and meeting places of every kind, attentive to the human needs of the inhabitants. Horse drawn carriages arrived and left with their passengers and the clip-clop of horse's hooves upon the cobblestones echoed through the streets. They continued through the darkened city until they came upon a wooded way which led to a parklike setting at the end of the last city street, and followed it down to a gently flowing stream. The way was lighted by torches which lined the wooded path. Crossing to the other side, the path led upwards to a bridge which crossed another stream and on the other side they found themselves in front of an ancient salon meeting place, and another stone step. Ascending onto the step at the ground floor of the three-story structure was a closed wooden door with no markings except a large brass handle through which they entered. Inside the structure, whose only external markings were a series of unintelligible symbols above the mantle of the door at the threshold, there lay before them a wooden staircase which they began to ascend.

Having ascended to the first floor, and entering, they sat and greeted the friends who were waiting for them. Students milled about, in turn waiting for the movement of their professor to begin the concert. Now the room became the great composer's chamber, whose instrument sat in the alcove by the windows overlooking the gardens below the old city salon. Polychromatic heliotherapy, using narrow band ultraviolet 312 nanometer radiations, continued the stimulation of his serotonergic neurons. Now his subconscious desire was for the ancient classical music played on period acoustic instruments, not driven by electricity and semiconductors. The sounds surrounded him as he floated in a fog of only near-consciousness. The cocktail of antidepressant mood enhancers provided by the girl who companioned him, relaxed Humboldt and brought on a drug induced dreamlike sequence. He was no longer the Population Control Director, nor was he any director, and no longer was he in control in any way. All was let go to the companion who had taken his hand with willing compliance, as she brought him out of the place in which he had been with his friends. Humboldt felt all fall away as the synthesized organic molecules entered his bloodstream. Amino acids rearranged themselves in hexagonal bridged structures attached to random nodes of a fullerene base compound, a sophisticated mind medicine which would leave no aftereffect, but was capable of producing intense, subconsciously stimulated, dreamlike sequences for short periods of time.

He was now the great master of ancient classical music while his companion, now his talented student, played and practiced for him in the main room of the music salon, on either side of which a room extended where casual audiences and aficionados alike could gather to celebrate the musical performances offered here.

He sat in the master's chair and evaluated and directed her playing, conducting the master class with his student. She was now somehow both reclining next to him and somehow still at the piano, in a movement as seamless as the playing from her hands. The musical notes flowed from his mind to her fingers as he sat and directed her silently. As she played, she moved to him and now up upon him, still playing, the masters chair both bed and pillowed, and they were surrounded and became part of the instrument – strings, keys, frame, and pedals intertwined with their bodies in a parody of the music itself. While he directed both her movements and her playing, he gazed at the garden outside which lay below the window. Sitting beside the piano at the same time he directed her playing from the bed and from the master's chair. The black and white key crescendos emerged and exploded and crushed, frightened and astonished the listeners who had followed the gentle beauty of their lyrical passage. His student followed the keys from base to treble and back again, from lightning to thunder, a three fingered double forte on the last black key.

He whispered to her as he held her to his side, his mouth to her ear and his lips upon her person as she both played and moved onto him, her hands moving up and down the keys, now his hands against her breasts as his mouth pressed more tightly against her. He bent over her, and her hands rushed up and down against him as if she were playing the keys of a desperate piano. He pushed against the music, the light, and her back as he spread her legs, closed his eyes and pressed the keys together against her, and went in and then down, down, down from treble to the depths of the base, and the three fingers still pushing heavily down on the last black key.

The drugs held them in an induced dream.

It was a sequence from which they arose – refreshed within their dream – he still in the master's chair while his student took a knowing bow to the audience in the salon. Together they retired to the music salon, always the music, and the sound, and the feeling. After, when the dream had fallen completely away, they lay together and relaxed before they arose from their resting place.

He began to rise to dress and leave the Flaxen Cafe to return home. "A flick of the wrist and the signal to the sensor," he thought, and she had appeared on his virtual demand, "and now in a moment she will be gone."

"Humboldt," she began, and turned to look at him, as randomly selected for her as for him, though she thought there was a brief hint of recognition. But it was too late for her initiation to be received. He had already fully awakened, turned to his own thoughts, and rose to leave her side. Perhaps it too was just an imitation of recognition within a drug induced dream sequence.

"I must begin to screen the applicants for spousal assignment number five," he said to himself, feeling the solitude now after the comfort and companionship of old friends, and another satisfying and creative STA encounter. He had long ago ceased to question the verisimilitude of anonymous encounters enhanced by the latest pharmacology. He smiled briefly to himself and thought of his friend, Alfrieda, the most compatible of his three closest friends, someone with beauty and emotional intelligence and a child already, someone with no immediate pressure to produce another human being.

He exited the glide path and walked to his building and entered. His thoughts turned again to the anonymous and perfectly free sexual and musical encounter he had just experienced.

"But still, she was most pleasant and perfectly beautiful," continuing his thoughts, "and with all the vitality of my still young age, my energy was directed with her own in a most satisfying way," he thought again and with no hint, however brief and fleeting, of recognition of the other, nor of a serious consideration for a spousal companion like Alfrieda.

vi

She awoke with a start, and with a satisfying ache deep within her she squeezed her thighs together, stretched her arms above her head until she could feel the muscles tighten the entire length of her torso. Now with an awakening consciousness she remembered the evening before at the Social Complex. Alfrieda Praxis lay with crossed arms above her head, the gentle breathing of sleep still remaining in the rise and fall of her breast, a slow awakening to full consciousness. There was no confusion or hesitation or wonder in her thoughts, or in memories of dreams from the evening before. She had participated in full consciousness, after she left her friends at the Flaxen, with no drug induced pleasures for the evening's therapy. Hers was a mind more mathematic than poetic, and though she had a love of literature, her profession was science based, and environmental science required objectivity and measurements first, with imagination and creativity as tools only to reduce the data to meaningful analysis. Data first. Emotion and desire would have to wait she told herself, and she struggled always to reconcile the two, because within her nature it was something to be reconciled.

It was an anomaly that always puzzled her. With only her second spousal partner she had wanted to have a child at the age of only one hundred seventy-three years. Of her friends, only Rotfach had selected a child at an earlier age, one hundred twenty-five, but that had been only through the demands of his spousal partner. He himself had little paternal interest in his first child. Nor did he take any particular interest in his second child by his fourth spousal partner.

"Open the S lights, please," she whispered, and the Seasonal Light Disorder lamps in the ceiling above the bed began to slowly illuminate and focus, and began to warm the bed coverings. She flung the bedclothes aside to feel the warmth of the light directly on the surface of her skin. She turned slowly from her back to her left side and as she did so, she examined the shape of her belly and below it the swelling of the iliac crest and how her thighs had not yet filled out the space between them. That there was still a pronounced protuberance tightening against her skin which fit into the palm of her right hand as she moved it down against her body, pleased herself.

"My body does not show signs of aging, yet," she thought to herself, thinking that only one third of her life was already lived at age three hundred twenty-three.

She rolled onto her stomach where she lay and felt the warmth of the lights against her buttocks and the small of her back, feeling her spine stretch and her shoulders relax and spreading her legs and tilting her pubis and pressing it against the mattress. Now onto her right side she rolled, feeling her belly pull away from her hip and permitting the light and the warmth to penetrate every inch of her body as she rolled again onto her back. She let the light shine on her face, breasts, stomach and abdomen. She felt it warm the entire length of her body from her abdomen down to her thighs and legs and to the tops of her feet as she stretched them downward, reaching as far out as she could as she pointed her toes out to the end of her bed, her light-colored hair pillowed beneath her. She closed her eyes which matched the color of her hair, her skin an almond glow beneath the lights, and she opened her eyes again.

She smiled as she remembered her three friends from the evening before at the Plex, and a satisfying murmur escaped her throat. She took a deep breath filling every space within her lungs and then slowly exhaled, grasped the pillow beside her, and remembering the encounter afterwards, clutched the pillow against her breast and belly and squeezed it between her thighs.

She sat up, drawing up her legs and crossing them as she did so, embracing the pillow with both her arms, pressing it against the emotionless expression on her unsmiling mouth, remembering with closed eyes. The warmth fading from the surface of the cloth. She opened her eyes as she lay back down again onto her back, letting the warmth of the light stay a few moments more on her face, breasts, stomach, hips, and legs.

"Please open the windows," she asked, and the filters of the polarized windows rotated and aligned themselves chemically within the glass so that she could see over the city, the dawn lightening the sky in the east as the glass became transparent to the view from inside her room. Her consciousness rose inside her. She remained hidden from view outside of the room as the sky lightened and another day began. She remained lying in the warmth of her bed as she awoke to full consciousness. She thought of Humboldt who had long ago become her best male friend at the university. For some reason their relationship had never become physical, though there had always been a kind of love between them.

"In earlier times, when we had only the length of one lifetime to live, we might have been different together," Alfrieda thought to herself.

But their friendship had been satisfying enough without the added sexual dimension, without the added complication, need, and desire of sex. Neither of them had insisted upon it, and in fact and perhaps because both had worried that it may have shortened their relationship, giving it spousal partner impermanence. By then the practice of sexual allowances had already been firmly established, and the consuming urges that would have been acted upon differently in earlier times, were satisfied by the STA's and temporary spousal partners of the new social order. Still, they had never parted their friendship in the decades that had already become centuries.

"Sometimes I feel to my regret," she thought.

Alfrieda was a scientist, and she accepted facts presented by science, including those facts that emphasized reason over emotion. She was, however a scientist of environmental concerns, and sometimes nature held emotions within its fact-based research. She knew that she and Humboldt had loved each other long before the first spousal partner was assigned to each of them. And after these so many years they still did love each other in their own ways, and she was sure they always would, perhaps one of the only few constants in their lives. They often spoke of it together.

"We are of the lucky ones," they both had thought.

"And we are able to share this transcendence through our fortunate and privileged long lives," she said to herself as she rose out of bed. The possibility of an enduring beauty the ancients were never able to attain.

She crossed the room and entered the bath. She stood in front of the mirror and recorded her daily measurements, standing erect with her hands to her sides. One hundred sixty centimeters, fifty kilograms.

"Humph," she thought, and straightened up a bit.

One hundred sixty-one. There should be no loss of height for many years yet to come. But she had no expectations that the weight would be close to the forty-eight kilograms she hoped for. That would be a struggle for the many years to come.

She removed her glance from the graphs of height and weight displayed on the mirror, frowned, and entered the water corner of the bath, dialed in the temperature, and chose the direction of the water flow; a spray of water from the side this morning, not from the rainfall orifice above. No need to wash my hair, she decided, and was already lost in environmental thought as the water splashed over her body. She lowered her face into the stream of wet warmth as it rose from her feet to the height of her shoulders, before descending to her feet and rising again repeatedly, as she stood against the spout of water. Her thoughts already turned to the Marine Isotope Stage analyses of warm and cold periods of Earth's MIS history, seismic projections, the close encounters of interplanetary orbiting objects, and singular interstellar masses briefly visiting our solar system. All of these, absent the technology of modern planetary protection shields, all were potential extinction events which had occurred repeatedly in the past four-plus billion years of the planet, when it emerged from the primordial chaos to the order that evolved within our present thirteen billion years old universe. On a scale of forward time which peered long enough into the future, any of these biotic crises were inevitable. The Confederation had called for a comprehensive plan to address these potentials. She stopped the flow of water and her thoughts continued. She often wished these problems could flow down and be carried away as easily as the water that washed over her body and disappeared into the drain in the floor.

"It is not yet time," she thought as she reached for the towel.

"It is not yet time," she hoped, as the peace drones slept on standby alert, though her own indefatigable mind could not rest.

vii

Konstantina Oblation had no such qualms of reflections or regrets on a night when she would share laughter and comradery with friends, and follow with a well-earned session with her chosen STA partner. Though she, like Alfrieda, had already experienced three spousal episodes, she was the kind of woman or man who took things as they were, did not agonize over alternatives not taken, and moved straight ahead with things as they came or as she tried to manage and control them. Believing herself not ready until she had been in her third spousal assignment, she felt then that the time was right for the one child she intended to have, and have one child she did, a healthy, happy girl who was now already approaching the fullness of her adult professional skills at the young age of eighty-seven. Konstance had given birth to her only child when she was still young in her early third century, at the age of two hundred nine. She was only forty years younger than her friend and colleague Humboldt, very close in age, and whose population control responsibilities had brought them together with questions concerning the legal ownership, property transfer rights, and other societal and personal obligations which were made increasingly complex as people's lives extended centuries, where once they were bound by decades. There were also difficult issues that held particular momentum in the discussions and debates between the lawyer and her friend Rotfach, the entrepreneur. She thought over their spirited conversation which had taken place earlier that evening.

"Yes, but why do the property rights of society mean that I have to give up some of the things I work for?" he would start his argument with. "If I must give up some of the things I have earned, then why is it society's decision how these are to be distributed?" intoned Rotfach, hoping to instigate a debate, or better yet, an argument.

"OK, here we go again," laughed Konstantina, "I'm going to take this one on once more," she continued, "as if you know what's best and how to control everything in your life and in ours!"

She laughed again, and turned to their other friends.

"Attention everyone, Rotfach is going to tell us how productive he is, and how dependent we are on his charitable intentions, and how best we should live on what he can afford to give up for the common good."

"That's not correct or fair," responded Rotfach. "I ask again, why is it society's right to distribute some of the things I have worked for that have been taken away from me by society? Why is it not my right to direct their distribution? I do think I know how best to make things work for the good of all, and particularly if we do not wish to upset the productivity of the people who actually work and produce the goods and services we need."

Sneering into the faces of his friends, he then turned to sit back triumphantly.

"But Rotfach, I agree, that is, that the property rights justification is proved if the incentive to work is rewarded when the proceeds from such work exceeds the cost input, or the sacrifices required to produce the work. Meaning that if there is a profit to the work performed. I also agree with you that the optimal amount of work that a society produces can't be attained absent property rights of owners and especially entrepreneurs such as yourself, entrepreneurs without which our society could not function, and without which I would have no profession."

This confession was particularly difficult for Konstantina, as a law partner, to admit. From her comfortable office, and from the sumptuous lairs from which many legal partners worked, was the belief that they had all earned the right to work. It was humbling of her to admit to Rotfach her own service role, and to remember just whom the customer was, and to whom it was that she was serving.

"I acknowledge the primary importance of your person in our society, Rotfach. But it is not only private property rights that are justified and necessary to provide the environment for productive work."

"What you are about to say is a distortion of my rights, and by the way I might add, even of the tribal rites of ancient man up until now. Your reasoning, and the rhetoric by which you express it, is a distortion of the rights of possession due the entrepreneurial risk takers that moved our civilization forward out of the darkness," Rotfach interrupted.

"Throw him a legbone of meat from the tribal rites of an ancient campfire," laughed Alfrieda. "He is on the hunt, and he is hungry for the kill. Please don't kill and eat me Rot. I still love you!"

"You laugh," he responded, "but seriously," he added, trying not to laugh himself, "try eating the meat off the bone raw, and you will begin to appreciate the ones who invented some of the things that allow our modern comforts and conveniences."

"But don't you acknowledge..." Konstantina tried to interject.

"What I acknowledge and what I even accept," he interrupted, "is that in the absence of property rights, the law of the jungle and the survival of the fittest emerges from the wilderness, the rule of law imposed by only the fittest among us applies, and the one who is not among the strongest will have to work a greater amount of time than is justified just for subsistence, because the strong will always take advantage of the weak, and the spoils of society will always be less fairly distributed without the rule of law."

"But surely," Konstantina countered, "you must accept that society itself has property rights in common for the means of production or services naturally owned by the Confederation. Things that exist for the common good, whether they be utilities, public safety, or transportation, etc. The work incentive in this kind of socialist organization can be fairly distributed with appropriate wages and benefits which reward good behavior, though the individual does not own, or even retain the right to own the actual output of his work, only the salaries and benefits representing the fair appraisal of the output of his work. It is only that which accrues to the individual worker who is part of a Confederation enterprise."

"In effect, that which accrues to a worker in either a Confederation-owned enterprise, or a privately owned enterprise is exactly the same. But for one, the profit accrues to the Confederation for the common good, and the other to the entrepreneur, who then must also share an appropriate amount of that profit to the Confederation for the common good."

"Yes, of course," answered Rotfach, "but I do not like the new property transfer regulations, which have been so called 'required' since the lengthening of lives. I find them odious in that they allow a final and irrevocable power to confiscate private property, and reallocate intellectual and real property ownership."

"Don't you recognize the confusion that would follow if private versus public property rights law had not evolved along with the lengthening of human lives?" Humboldt interjected.

"Even the decrees that brought all legally recognized individuals into the Confederation Uinkaret, you can argue, were confiscatory, and anti-individual, but necessary for the orderly progression of man. There would be no fair chance – I did not say equal chance – of ownership by the younger citizens," Humboldt intoned, "without the evolving Law of Distribution and Social Order."

It was on these points that Humboldt's relationship with the lawyer Konstantina had naturally developed. The LDSO was a principle on which the social order depended, and the citizens were rewarded with comfort, health, and safety, to encourage and support interesting and meaningful lives, in exchange for what it was necessary to sacrifice for the common good.

"I still don't like it," grumbled Rotfach, "and without my company, which is now solely owned by society, a social corporation which holds my contract, we would not be having this conversation. I do not like the feeling that I am forced to be a reluctant socialist despite my entrepreneurial preferences, because my company is owned by the Confederation, over my not-yet-dead body," he concluded.

"It is not in the manner in which the company was formed, and is not consistent with the founder's independent drive and spirit," he added for a final emphasis.

And so on, and so on, and so on, thought Konstantina. The living and breathing and renewed daily stresses. Perhaps what keeps life fresh – to question, debate, and be forced to reaffirm the way in which we live in order to progress towards the future we collectively choose. But she was now weary from the day and the conversations she was sometimes unable to let go. She had not only a photographic memory, courtesy of her parents and a desired genetic engineering edit which was statistically only directional in the preference for certain wished for traits, but she also possessed a Highly Superior Autobiographical Memory that sometimes disallowed her sleep. Too much HSAM information, she thought as she tried to clear her mind. It was possible within the time spent in the act with an STA partner, to forget all that was around her. Now she was alone, back in her apartment. She had a fleeting desire to talk to her daughter, and always wondered about it when she occasionally had this feeling. She did not question it. They were both more intellectual and only somewhat emotional. But there was still a kind of love and respect between them that she and her daughter held onto. It was of the flesh, not centered in the mind.

Think about it, she told herself. Rotfach had a point, but there was the common good. It made her laugh to think of him as a socialist. He was not pleased at the accreditation. Life was long now, there were still memories and stories of decades which had turned to centuries, but there were still fleeting moments of life's daily intensity, and the brevity of even these brief moments. All the images and the sounds of the day came back to her and rushed against her consciousness in competition with her body, until her physical being took over her mind, and she soon fell asleep, freed temporarily from the onrush of every picture and sound which informed her conscious being of every waking hour.

viii

Rotfach Theoretrics had not in fact left the Flaxen with his evening's companion. They had shared a drink together with the other three couples, but had only a brief conversation before Rotfach had turned him away. It was not that he was particular about the sex of an STA companion. He was not. Random or chosen, he did not care. But tonight, he had other things on his mind, and the physical entertainment that he so often needed, like all other healthy citizens of the Confederation, was not the one that would satisfy him tonight. Sex was considered just another bodily function by him. But there were other things troubling him this night, and his irrepressible energy had only masked it earlier in the evening, an evening that he had enjoyed immensely with his friends. It was not enough to continue with a ruse, however, and he knew that the concerns with which his old friend Humboldt had come to the Flaxen Cafe, were also his own concerns. He did not want to and could not speak about these things that evening with his friends. He had hoped that they would be forgotten during the moments they spent together in friendship, comradery, refreshments, entertainment, and the satisfying debate and arguments of the evening. But these concerns had not gone away by the conclusion of the evening's fest, and by the time his three friends left with their companions for the remainder of the evening, he knew that he needed to work, and that only work would suffice his needs.

Rotfach often teased his friends about the business output that his company produced, compared to the function of bureaucrats and academics, but in fact he respected their professions as equally as his own. It was just that commerce, and especially technologically-based production commerce, was the driving force of his life. His work gave meaning to his life; he lived to work, to produce, and to apply the technology developed by his company to produce goods used to make the society of his Confederation possible. Humboldt had often told his old friend Rotfach, that he believed the son or daughter he hoped for would make the world a better place, and that he did in fact believe the world would be a better place with the birth of his hoped-for child. Above all, Humboldt also wished for a son or daughter to be fulfilled as a human being no matter what they chose to do, and to be satisfied with just who they were. For Rotfach though, it was his own work that he believed in, his own work that would make the world a better place, and he did not feel the ache of parental love in the same way his friend Noraxton imagined, even though he already had two children, and Humboldt had not yet had his first child. Already the father of two children, Rotfach no longer felt the desire to make another new life together with another spouse, another feeling, thinking, working human being, no matter how accomplished in their own right they might be. He no longer desired to make a commitment to the care with which both he and his spousal partner would have to make to choose the characteristics of another offspring and raise that child to adulthood. It was not that he was a solitary man, he had friends of both sexes, and relationships with one or another without discrimination. And though he had experienced more spousal partners than his three closest friends – five relationships and two children – it was not his children's beings or needs which drove him, but rather his own in an unbalanced desire that drove his singular genius. He doubted that though only a third of his life had been lived, would he seek a sixth spousal partner, nor would he ever want another child. He wanted to dedicate the rest of his life to his work. His friendships, the Flaxen Café, and the STA Clubs were now enough to fulfill a life for himself outside of work.

At the beginning of the new Fifty-Year Plan, early in the year 9,950, Rotfach and his company were directed to begin planning for the Great Migration. This was not just to be an enhancement of the permanent Martian settlement which already existed on the fourth planet. This was to be a project requiring the highest level of security clearances, to be staffed in the initial planning stages with the best minds of industry and academia to produce what would be a broad outline, a comprehensive first level Gantt chart mapping the requirements of a new human survival. This was to be a new human evolution, not a mutating rearrangement and building up of base pair nucleotides on an increasing complex double helix chain of protein assembly instructions. No, this was not to be an event evolving over eons of time, like that of the third planet's history. This, the first man-made evolution of the Earth's human species, in this one of many billions of solar systems in our galaxy, one of countless galaxies in the present universe. This, an evolution not directed by a chemical, intracellular genetic mutation in response to some external stimulus. This would be the first evolution directed by the consciousness of the organism itself.

We were going to go to Mars in a way in which it would be impossible to return to the world we would leave behind.

Virtual reality now existed for the Confederation's Earth society as a necessary tool of monitor and control. This, in fact, was already in place for the limited, and still primarily scientific, settlement on Mars. But this migration alone would be a technological and engineering feat. Nor, if graphed, would it represent a linear extension of Earth's primacy to man. No, this line was to be inscribed on a new page. Rotfach's task was to produce the first of a series of comprehensive plans to make

Mars a second Confederation society, a complete autonomous human world not dependent on Earth support. An exponential advance. A second society of equals. Equal lifeboats to the other, in defense of the inevitable next K-T extinction event which was ever and always inevitable in a frequency measured in the magnitude of space time. Were we to be capable of this greatest feat of humanity and engineering, perhaps we could see our way to other solar systems within our Milky Way Galaxy and extend our chance and destiny of survival to other new worlds, and in the fullness of the time scales of the universe, perhaps to spread humanity beyond the galaxy in which we had begun to exist – to extend the digital, chemical, life rendering of our DNA, across the vast expanse of the present known universe?

"That may be the goal," he thought to himself, "but the work to achieve the result is only begun," catching himself before he, too, was carried away.

"Perhaps the dreamers have decided our future," his thoughts continued, "but they are not capable of imagining the design or engineering required to complete it, the complexities and risks to be overcome which will be required to perhaps even exceed the cumulative achievements of man."

"Perhaps it is not even begun, and if it is only the conception of a beginning, what may lie ahead if it cannot be completed?" he shuddered to think.

He retreated to the study in his apartment, the view from the window overlooking the gleaming city which his company had helped create. The first faint traces of dawn appeared on the horizon in the east. He opened the transparency of the windows to the highest aperture so that the appearance of the glass in front of him became almost invisible, and he felt as if he could float in the absence of gravity out over the city. For a few moments which became minutes of quiet contemplation, he sat in front of the window and looked out over this political landscape which he had helped build. Then, needing solitude and a separateness, he commanded the windows to dim, and he shut out the emerging dawn. The chemical molecules imbedded within the glass aligned themselves again in perpendicular patterns that gradually filled in all the spaces on the surface of the film within the panes of glass. Rotfach now sat in darkness but for the light that illuminated the surface of his desk. He activated a holographic display screen, and at the same time placed a pad of polymerized paper on the desk, and opened a writing utensil with which he began to apply against the paper and which recorded his marks – words and graphs and drawings automatically appeared on the screen. He began to work. He could feel the sense of history within him and in his thoughts, and he allowed a stream of consciousness to express itself simultaneously on paper and on the holographic display, a way in which he often began his creative process. He could feel the sense of responsibility assigned to himself and the Great Migration team, and imagined what the founder of his company, Markus Funk, had felt when he, too, was faced with a turning point in the history of man's achievements. Hours passed as the papers accumulated and the displays were archived as he worked through the hours of early dawn.

By midmorning Rotfach, with many hours of work yet to complete, felt that something small was wrong in the space around him in which he found himself intensely working. He commanded the windows to transparency, raised his eyes off the pages and the displays, and looked out over the cityscape. After a few moments, as if refreshed from the view beyond his desk and window, and the meaning that lay herein, he again lowered his eyes to the task in front of him, and continued the struggle with words, and graphs, and drawings – and the collecting-all of mathematics.

For the first time he grasped and truly felt the meaning of the work in which he was engaged. There would be no going back now, there could be no going back now, there would be no second guessing except in the design and the method of the actions upon which they would execute. The space in which he worked – the comfort, convenience, and familiarity –

would be offered up in the solutions it was given to him and his company to devise. He was to design himself to redundancy, he was to plan his own demise or escape. He did not know which would be the day or the hour that the result of the plans and actions would be demonstrated into the substance of reality.

He pushed back his chair, rose, and stood in front of the glass which separated him from the city outside. Rotfach was not an emotional man but he was an aggressive man, his intellect worked off of reason and logic, and he seldom expressed anything more than impatience and intensity, and the spirited debates he liked to engage in with his friends. He could be a very argumentative man. The migration to a new world excited his intellect and opened up his curiosity, and he knew he would meet the challenge with the passion and strength of all his skill and ability. But there was more to it than mere commercial and professional success. He suddenly felt it in the smallest molecular meaning, the thing he carried in each cell of his body. The survival of the essence of life itself, and not just the beautiful spaces in which man had managed to create for himself in which to live and learn, and carry-on human history. He could feel it in the meaning of his forty-six chromosomes in twenty-three pairs, the passport to life and the only true way in which it was defined what it meant to be human, and the method by which we truly survived the generations, extending back through the eons to the prokaryotic last universal ancestor. Rotfach felt the passing of that time rush upon himself from the Archean Eon's rise of life, to his own mindful musings, before the window which separated him from the life of the city below.

His was the task to protect, and defend, and permit the continuation of procreation itself, of the more than three billion base pairs of nucleotides that defined our species.

From the smallest of the spaces within himself, there arose the understanding of the immensity of the task set before him. His eyes rose from the city beyond the window, to the sky above, and down again to his hands, turning them over and back and over again to look at the decimal of math that his ten fingers represented, the mystery of their meaning and evolution. He moved back away from the window, sat down, and began again to write and draw on the papers. He let his design thoughts flow from his mind to the stylus against the papers from which his marks were captured and computerized into the three dimensional holographic displays which surrounded him.

"To survive the generations," he thought to himself.

"The means by which we survive the generations," he repeated this thought to himself again.

III
ARK

i

The Great Cataloging Activity (TGCA) had begun in the ninety-eighth century. Over nine million known species of flora and fauna existed in the oceans and on the Earth. Developments in gene sequencing technology became so advanced that the physical seed archives of the ancients, once scanned and sequenced, were no longer needed to be retained in archives of physical storage which had been maintained at great cost, and a never fully integrated risk. A scientific compendium of a book of life was the goal, a repository of life science, of DNA reduced and mapped from the chromosomes of every living organism. With a database so vast, and with machine intelligence so capable, expectations of understanding the structure of life itself was the goal. Decoding the mystery of the way in which the double helix of every living organism was programmed into four simple nitrogen-based molecules, chemically linked together with weak hydrogen bonds of non-covalent interactions, became the mantra of a new desire for the most basic human wisdom of all – to approach an understanding of the meaning and source of life. A great asymptotic journey of discovery and survival, and an application of the most advanced and modern technological analysis was begun. But an asymptote never arrives to its ultimate destination, though in distance it becomes infinitely closer, and in spite of the fact that we were destined to succeed in the re-creation of life, the mystery would remain as to where and how the first application of this knowledge had occurred. That is, how did life itself begin? And though an understanding of the creation of the universe fourteen billion years earlier, with the explosive escape of energy and matter from the Great

Black Hole was well theorized, what was it that existed before the creation of our universe came to be? What came before, and before, and before, and then after, and after, and after – as in the unending reflection contained within two mirrors placed in front of one another where the images of the object between them reflect back and forth to go on as an asymptote towards forever? Are these the images of our future or the images of our past?

It was understood that in the one hundred to perhaps two-hundred-year timeline of the vast cataloging project, technology would change so that in every generational shift, a re-programming would need to take place to recapture all that had been previously sequenced and translated into a new storage medium. This resulted in a series of redundant, obsolete archives as the work progressed. Layers of this repetitive data suggested a resemblance to the repetitive gene sequencing of common genetic data that is shared across all species. This is to say, the genetic instruction for basic life activities exists at the molecular level for the order in which the physical structure of all organisms develop. The genes containing these basic instructions are conserved, they are the homologous genes representative and similar for many of the basic life processes of any living organism, like the laying out of a complex body plan complete with a central nervous system. These are the basic genetic instructions which remain largely unchanged in the process of evolution. In the minds of some scientists, data redundancies in the genetic information of a life form's DNA structure occur where streams of data seem to repeat themselves over and over again with only slight variation, as if the record of life started and stopped and started again. And it was discovered that a relatively small portion of the total DNA information distinguishes one species or individual from another. That there are more similarities in the genetic code between individuals of our species than differences – 99.9% of the three billion plus genetic base pairs that make up the human genome are identical – demonstrating that this commonality is what makes us the family of human beings. Leaving only three million base pairs with which to differentiate ourselves from one another and make each person an individual, it remains at the genetic level that we are all more alike than we are different, a knowledge long understood by the ancients in their wisdom, knowing only the truth of what we are, and not the why and the how. A wisdom achieved by the empirical observation of human nature in the absence of technological science.

In this century, at the end of ten thousand years of human history, the technology to recreate life in its most basic form, from the information contained in a DNA sequence, was developed.

The responsibilities for Humboldt now included the science of Life Control. The giant leap in technology had been to enable the creation of single and multi-celled creatures. It was only a matter of time before science could achieve the creation of a drosophila common fruit fly, with already one-half the number of human genes, and one twentieth the number of human nucleotides. It was only a matter of time before man himself could be understood by science. It had taken three billion years for the last universal ancestor to appear on Earth and develop through genetic selection before it shook the hand of man. Then only another one hundred centuries for man to master the science of the three-billion-year-old technology of nature called DNA.

Science had dissected the math and the chemistry. What still remained, mined in the depths of poetry and the arts, was the mystery of life itself.

DNA. And then all was to be lost on Earth. It was the inevitable truth.

The leaders of the Confederation understood the environmental signs that were emerging and began to alter the Fifty-Year Plan. The nine million species of flora and fauna had been identified since the 98th Century when genetic mapping had begun in earnest. It was known that the creatures of eons past which once roamed the Earth until lost in the great K-T extinction event had lived in a too distant past, and so foreign to the modern world that there was little mourning for those lost life forms of the millions of years past, mere scientific interest, archaeologic and paleontological curiosities, with no need to replicate in a new world. DNA, first life, and photosynthesis arose in the first two billion years of the planet. Geologic and celestial events, and natural selection defined the third and fourth billion years. Now it was man's choice to help enable a new selection process.

Among the first tasks of a proposed Project Haven would be to require that redundant repositories of the TGCA record of life on Earth be taken to the Autonomous Resettlement Kolony and dispersed for safety in different geographical locations on Mars. In addition to the planet-based repositories, one repository would remain to sail in perpetuity at the outer reaches of the solar system between the seventh and eighth planets, captured in a one hundred-five-year orbit around the sun. It would be a last lifeboat, a final chance, a scapegoat for the absolution of the potential innocence contained within a spacecraft orbiting our sun.

It was agreed that it would take at least ten thousand vehicles for the flights to the Mars settlement just to provide the means to establish the minimum infrastructure required to sustain life independently for the first two Martian generations. Then it would be up to the ingenuity of man to make a new world. Two generations, the period of only two lifetimes. Perhaps a couple of millenniums were the lives of the colonists to be sustained for the full measure of their lengthened years. The thinnest veneer of life sustained and dependent only upon the will of man's ability to survive. The Confederation agreed that the provision for two generations was necessary in order to give man the opportunity to re-establish a successful and permanent society in the new world.

Launches would take place on a rotating basis, ten launch days per month, every third day, and two launches per days of flight. All ships, life and cargo, would be equipped with self-guidance systems to manage the space craft on the journey to the next planet in the solar system. If in a straight line, a journey of eighty million kilometers. No flight crews would accompany the ships. Because it takes more than twice as long on its synodic path around the sun for the planet Mars to orbit the sun as it does for our own planet Earth to journey around the sun on its near circular orbit, only close-orbit launches were possible for life ship launches from Earth to Mars, in order to keep the human mission lengths to approximately eight months. It meant that the launch periods for cargo versus human/flora/fauna flights would be staggered. In the twenty-six-month synodic period of revolution, the time required for the two planets to lap one another, launches for life versus cargo flights would rotate on an eight to nine-month schedule. These launch schedules would be timed so that life flights would coincide with opposition of the planets, that period in their synodic orbits when they would they would be at their closest approach and on the same side of the sun. Cargo launches would be timed to arrive at Mars closest to conjunction, when the planets aligned themselves at their farthest approach, at opposite sides of the sun. The cargo launches would take approximately three months longer than a life ship launch to reach the planet Mars, orbiting the sun and moving from the eastern quadrature to the western quadrature in the more than two years it takes for the planet to complete its orbital journey, relative to the Earth. Nine months on and nine months off, for the rotation of life versus cargo flights, in a race to achieve the second Confederation on the fourth planet.

All of this was discussed within the Fifty-Year Plan established in year 9950, the plan to bring man to the close of the hundredth century and usher in a new millennium. Contingency planning had to be acknowledged and expected to be required, knowing that at only twenty massive launches per month it would take forty-two years to complete a migration to Mars. Concurrent Engineering would need to be used for as yet unknown processes, capabilities, and the unforeseen problems which would inevitably arise. A forty-plus year timeline would need to be compressed over time, perhaps to twenty years or less after the initial launches took place, were significant environmental dangers to arise on Earth early in the min-max slope graph of probability curves. Were a disastrous shift to the left to occur in the probability curves, it would mean quickly ramping up to a seemingly impossible eight launches per every third launch day. CE held more risk, but it was the only way to engineer and achieve results in an impossibly compressed time schedule.

A 2% failure rate at launch, during the flight to Mars, or during entry, decent, and landing was reluctantly decided acceptable. It was hoped that this mission rate failure would be less, but the contingency for it had to be recognized and provided for in the project guidelines. There could, however, be no allowance for excessive redundancy, and it was accepted that genetic knowledge had progressed to such a degree that the actual living organism need not always be saved, if the genomic mapping was concluded in sufficient detail that life could be re-created. To be able to accomplish that meant that this genetic technology, along with other essential technologies and documentation related to its use, would need to be transferred along with any infrastructure needed to support it. Significant technology was already in place at the permanent Mars settlement where much had been learned and was positioned for further development. There had been much spirited debate on the advocacy of cargo technology infrastructure flights versus life flights, and balancing the need for the survival of technology to ensure the survival of the human organism.

This was the question that the highly evolved man in the one hundredth century of recorded history was forced to ask himself.

"At what point is life worth living? Are we even capable of life without the substantial technological infrastructure required to prevent the devolution of our lengthened human lifespan and our comparatively advanced civilization?"

ii

The slanting rays of the sun settled over the wide Quaternary Uinkaret Plaza, the largest open space within the city. The warmth of the stone pavers, set into what appeared at first glance to be simple geometric patterns, formed complex, non-repeating shapes, as if these were caricatures of prime and Fibonacci numbers. The retained heat of these stone pavers would soon give up their energy to the cooling air, and the colors and shapes of the city structures and the surrounding countryside would move, shift, and change. Humboldt Noraxton's footsteps created a quiet but solid aural trail as he crossed the immense space, a satisfying sound, the solidity of the city's expression affirmed with each step he took.

He was walking towards the building which rose out of the center of the plaza. The entire structure of the building was shaped like two pyramids connected at their bases. But as one approached the building, only one of the pyramids was visible above ground. Though he was not able to perceive it and detect the direction of it, the sound of each footfall reflected off the side of the crystal triangle capping the pyramid which faced in his direction, and reflected upward to be dispersed into the open sky.

The building consisted of one pyramid above ground, and one pyramid below, with the bases of the pyramids at ground level. Within it the most powerful leaders of the Uinkaret were now seated at the deepest level of the buried inverted pyramid, which led down into a four-sided triangular chamber which contained the smallest rows of seats of the inverted apex, the four rows facing the center where a speaker's lectern stood.

The Fifty-Year Plan had been debated for months within the Great Hall of the Interplanetary Confederation after years of preplanning. Humboldt took his seat in the pyramid's third tier, waiting to address his colleagues present in the Great Hall's chamber. Before him the elected and selected managerial and senatorial leaders of all parties were present.

Around Humboldt and above him, sat the succeeding layers of support and organizational professionals. The open four-sided pyramid rose from ground level above the last and largest row of seats of the Interplanetary Chamber. The upper pyramid's great square base was placed on top of the seats of the open chamber's descending amphitheater. Rising above ground, the four huge triangles of the upper chamber met to a crystal pyramidion at the highest point, far above the seats lining the concentric rows below where all the members sat. The pyramid above brought all eyes to the transparent ben-ben at the apex above them, and below, upon the stage where the members made their speeches. From deep within the lower pyramid chamber, Humboldt rose from his third-tier seat and ascended the stage to take his place at the lectern, an illuminated holographic text surrounded him.

"Senators and colleagues," Humboldt began, "it is time."

He paused and looked out and up over the assembled citizens. Silence blanketed the audience which surrounded him in every direction as he turned his body first to the left, and then to the right, the only sound, the movement of the fabric of his clothing as he came back to center his gaze. A breath, and then he continued.

"During our ten thousand years of recorded history, humankind has brought themselves through the warming phase which ended almost fifty centuries ago. For the past thirty centuries we have experienced the new blooming, the climate adjusting to moderating temperatures, having moved past the peak of Earth's current warming phase. We are now in the next cooling phase, and we have also increasingly detected seismic activity related to the turn of this climatology."

"While we believe the environmental risks are manageable in the short term measured in centuries, we must be prepared to act and plan accordingly while we have sufficient time for our imaginations and ingenuity to guide us and inform us. We must act and grasp the responsibilities we have to maintain and protect our modern world here at the Uinkaret, while at the same time promoting the advance of a new society to be fully formed at our Martian outpost. Optimally, two societies in a symbiotic relationship are what we strive for, is what we would like our next destiny to be – the new world and the old world, in proximate orbits around our mother sun."

"Dear colleagues and friends, perhaps it is only fitting that as we complete the repository of the genetic codes of all life forms on Earth, we are poised on a new trajectory, the purpose of which is to protect and extend the knowledge gained in this, The Great Cataloging Activity."

"It is therefore incumbent upon us to acknowledge publicly our desire to make the second society on Mars a fully functional and equal partner in our now twice human solar system."

"We are announcing today the commencement phase of ARK – the Autonomous Resettlement Kolony on Mars – moving forward from the planning stage after the completion of The Great Cataloguing Activity. It is an endeavor which will require the skills and support, the dedication and the treasure of all our citizens as we move to make a general colonization of the fourth planet, to extend the mining and permanent settlement operations, long established there, to a fully functional and freely independent society, and to bind together the two societies of our planets by the representation of the Interplanetary Confederation."

"I hereby declare, in this great hall, the establishment of permanent articles of a joint Constitution for the two interplanetary societies now bound to one common Confederation. With this declaration, we announce that we will no longer be alone in this solar system, dependent on only one world within which we are all bound with an unalienable right to promote our human existence. We pledge our wealth, our honor, and our future lives to both of our worlds, to our mother Earth, and to the new settlement which we hereby announce, Project Haven."

"Now and forever, we are joined by the strength, promise, and the history of three billion years of DNA, from the prokaryote of the last universal ancestor of early Earth history until today. With the actions we declare here, at the present now, that the procreation of the twenty-three pairs of our forty-six chromosomes will now and forever survive and flourish and become part of two worlds, not one, to spring forth again from Earth to Haven, forever and ever."

"The sacrifices required from our society in this age will be a testament to the vision and strength of the human mind and the unending desire to explore and experience new frontiers of knowledge and to expand human understanding into never ending new technologies and to the rightful progression of human life."

With that, the Director of Population Control, Humboldt Noraxton, allowed the image of his speech grow dark, as his last words faded from the illuminated text before him, left the podium, and took his seat in the Assembly's third tier. There was silence in the great hall for a few moments except for the sound of his footsteps as he crossed and exited the stage. Then a rising tide which began in timorous whispers, became the resounding chorus and a rising crescendo of white noise which emanated from the seated listeners, who in a moment were now standing. The chorus of the voices ascended to the oculus of the pyramidical structure which rose above them, rising to the highest point above the seated assembly. The sound reflected back down from the ben-ben of the crystal pyramidion as if were the igniting single clap of a phoenix bird, reflected over and over by the acoustic echoes within the architectural pyramid.

iii

Rotfach Theoretrics left the Great Hall and took the glide path past the offices of Rundfunk. It was late afternoon and the sun had already passed from its highest point in the southeastern sky to begin its southwestward journey to the horizon. Against the distant mountains of the Uinkaret the colors began to change as the angle of the sun refracted the light in a changing motion, and he imagined the descending wavelengths of the photons which had journeyed eight minutes from the surface of the sun to create the southern exposure on the distant mountains. In an unfolding mystery after mystery of nature, Rotfach reflected on the fact that prior to the eight-minute journey of the photons to our planet, they had already traveled for a hundred thousand years within the boiling cauldron of the sun's interior before they reached the surface of the sun. From its inner core where they were formed, colliding billions of times per second in random directions against the sun's atomic structures, they migrated to the surface of the sun. An unimaginatively violent birth provided the source of energy for life on Earth to develop. In the three billion years since the rise of the last universal ancestor and DNA, how many times had the genetic nucleotides opened and separated and rejoined again in the unending random ballet of life? Perhaps there would be another two billion years before the sun's increasing intensity would bake the life out of planet Earth and any other life in the solar system. Was it mere human folly to establish a second society on Mars to increase the chances of interplanetary survival before the final solar extinction? To enable survival until man's technology advanced enough to escape even the eventual sun death with a leap from interplanetary to interstellar space survival? It had taken man ten thousand years to be able to leap from planet to planet, a fraction of the time it takes a photon to reach the surface of the sun and emerge. How many thousands or millions of years would need to pass in order to devise an interstellar leap?

As he approached his residence, Rotfach watched as the colors of the mountains changed, now reflected against the dichroic coated glass walls of the building, a technology of multi-layered metallic vapor deposition invented and developed by his company centuries earlier, one small step in the advancement of thermal protection and efficiency, a small building block for the new world of the Uinkaret. He could not help but think of the way things were made and constructed. His mind worked to construct and deconstruct the things he saw around him. It was a curiosity and an imperative for him to understand the natural world in order to design and construct by the laws of nature. Less so for the man-made legal and societal order. That was what his other friends were for.

If his purpose was to understand the laws of nature, so as to enable his efforts to build and to make nature habitable for man, the task for his friends was to establish the order and governance of the very things without which we could not live, and the ways in which we interacted with one another in our deconstructed nature-derived, then man-made artifice of our reconstructed world.

His shadow fell against the windowed face of his building. While he entered his home, the members of the Confederation were still discussing the activities of the latter purpose in the Great Hall which he had left earlier that afternoon. These were the discussions which he had left behind for the others to consider. His interest this day was only in the decision that had already been made years before, but announced publicly only today. There was no need for him to participate in additional debate. His entire conscious and unconscious being was now focused on action, not words.

It had always seemed easier for him to address nature and its embedded mathematics, and for his friends to address the nature of man.

"The processes by which man built the world in which we live. All was derived from nature, all understanding rooted in the scientific and technological learning of man, and applied within the natural world to provide a home for all of us in which to live," he thought.

"Twenty-three pairs of chromosomes brought us here, and now there will be two worlds," he said quietly to himself as he entered his flat.

Konstantina Oblation did not leave the Great Hall early, as had her great debating friend, Rotfach. Lawyer that she was, she knew that she had a professional obligation to, and in fact would have it no other way than to hear all of the speeches of the assembled leaders of the now "Interplanetary" Confederation. After the speeches had concluded, and the assembled had met their leaders with applause, she left the hall surrounded by the legal colleagues at her side, in front, and behind her. They exited the cojoined pyramids of the hall, moving like a human ship through the chamber's broad entrance promenade, and ascending a carved stone staircase, exited the architectural tour de force. Starboard, port, forward, aft – to set sail to the ARK and Haven. They walked out of the glass and steel entrance pyramid that led up onto the plaza and beyond that of the boulevard of the Confederation, a wide expanse in the city center, the twin pyramids of the Confederation rising from the north side, facing south, one a great granite base structure buried beneath the surface, the other rising above the plaza, sheathed in quartz glass, both made of silicone dioxide. Materials of the Earth's formation, these had been pushed out of their tectonic plate, raised by fracture propagation into the batholith of the plutons of the mountain ranges surrounding the Uinkaret. One structure made of nature's opaque material, granite. The other of nature's material converted by man to become transparent, pure, silicone dioxide quartz. Both of these structures represented the history of humankind's ability to utilize nature.

The group of lawyers gathered, still in the setting southeastern sunlight on the wide plaza, but Konstantina chose to go on alone, taking leave of her colleagues and friends. With each step on the stones of the plaza she thought of her daughter, and of the great task before them, and of the terrible responsibility that would be left to her to present her recommendations to the DPC, to her friend Humboldt, the Director of Population Control. She knew the terrible, difficult discussions that the Control would have to make for the Mars missions, and the limits which would be imposed upon those chosen to be the new pioneers of Mars. To decide who would continue on, and who would not. Of the four million inhabitants of the Uinkaret, she had already calculated that with ten thousand total flights to Mars, of which two thousand would be comprised of human cargo, it meant that only twenty thousand men, women, and children would be able to take the journey to the planet, one half of one percent, a tiny fraction of Uinkaret inhabitants, with almost all left behind to face the potential end of Earth as it was known. It would mean that any parent with an adult child would have no chance to go on to the new world with his child. It meant that any woman of child bearing age selected for the Mars Haven mission would be required to bear as many children as possible once arrived on the fourth planet whether natural or from the stores of frozen blastocysts. And that both women and men must be chosen for both physical strength and intellectual capacity, prepared for an environment both environmentally and physically harsh, with a constant stress on the need to demonstrate and execute physical, creative, intellectual, and technological success – or perish.

Should Konstantina's child be among the chosen, would that child and her children forever be lost to her on a distant planet? Was her child not to be among the chosen, would she meet an uncertain fate linked to her mother's own Uinkaret destiny?

It would be planned that the twenty thousand colonists would grow to a new four million. A two-hundred-fold increase. Assuming sufficient resources and an absence of pestilence, war, or self-destruction, such an increase would be possible within a span of four ancient lifetimes, four hundred years. That would be in the near distant future, but still a future in which no one who remained on Earth might be left alive to see.

Konstantina Oblation wanted to make her way home to see if her daughter were available for a late-night conversation. A beautiful child, Zabana was now a beautiful adult. Among the genetic traits she had chosen for her daughter were those of Taino origin, from an ancient indigenous people's race, one of the earliest societies of tall, athletically strong, beautifully hued and proportioned peoples. A standout among her peers. Now she wanted to hear her daughter's voice, to ask about her day, her plans, and to hear her say, "I love you," and to tell her so in return.

She entered her apartment, turned to close the door, and asked that the shutters of the floor to ceiling glass be opened. Without asking that any interior light be opened as well, she sat and looked through the glass to the view of the city before her, and beyond to the mountains in the distance. In the field of view of a waning gibbous moon, a bright bluish-green star, Mars, glowed above and to the left of the luminous disk. Gentle shadows cast shapes on the floor of the room. She turned to the table beside her, and touched the tiny metal sculptures suspended on the tiny metal armature. The little legs danced as they swung back and forward, moved by the tip of her finger, as if drawing a mallet across the bars of a windchime, but one that made no sound. As silent as the bluish-green star of Haven before it disappeared into the menstruum of dawn.

The senate session Rotfach had left early did not inspire him as much as fill him with a sense of regret. He had not remained in the chamber to hear the speeches that would follow that of his friend, Humboldt Noraxton. He had no desire to listen to the platitudes and congratulatory words of those ministers who easily took credit for the work of the people who actually performed the tasks ordered by the Confederation, the work of he and his colleagues at Rundfunk. Older than his three closest friends, at three hundred seventy-eight years of age, one third of Rotfach's life had already passed, perhaps as much as one half if he looked at what was still the median attained age of seven hundred years, and not the fully possible one thousand years. He hoped that he would have at least a thousand years to work and learn and develop and build, whether here on this planet or on the new, second world that was about to begin. He wondered what thoughts were in the minds of his friends Humboldt, Alfrieda, and Konstantina. He knew that in many ways they did not share the emotional intensity of his passions, and perhaps because of this they had more balanced aspects to certain parts of their lives. There were so many things which generated no passion in him, or even preference, whether sexual, the surroundings in which he lived or worked, the food he ate, or the two children he had fathered. For many of these basic needs he had no firm preference. For him it was work that drove his passion, and the end of work was to him the end of life. He had felt a strange sense of hopelessness and emptiness

on the glide path that had carried him past Rundfunk, at a time
when the hope for society expanded with the addition of a
second world, a world he would help design and set in motion.
The greatest migration in human history, like seeds that
survived ocean crossings and planted themselves in new islands
and continents of ages past, the age of man was poised after two
billion years of life ascendancy to sail across an interplanetary
emptiness to make another new, blue world, his own.

He addressed the glowing screens suspended in front of him,
surrounded   by   three   dimensional   representations   of
probabilities. He vowed to himself that his work not become an
elegy to life on Earth, but instead the technology of a new birth
which required an acceptance of the possibility of death, even
the death of a planet in order to survive. And he imagined a tiny
spacecraft as if ejaculated from the gravity of his own planet
Earth, propelled upon the streaming exhaust tail of its rocket
engine as it passed through the bounds of the Earth's
atmosphere, ejected into space, coursing through the near
perfect vacuum with the occasional trailing tail of a hydrazine
thruster flight correction jet, the craft's only purpose to cross
inhospitable space, enter the gaseous atmosphere of a new
world, and implant itself onto the surface to establish new life.

"The image of a new conception," Rotfach said quietly, to
no one but himself.

iv

Before the Great Migration could begin, construction of the
Great Migration Space Port would take place, to increase the
launch capability of the present engineering and civil defense
space facility. Two launch facilities would be built to
accommodate the ten thousand flights to Mars. The Robotic
Mission Launch Facility, the RMLF for the unmanned cargo
launches, and the Human Spaceflight Launch Facility, the
HSLF for the manned space flights. These would be built on
the broad plain surrounding the city, anchored on the stable
base of the three hundred-million-year-old Kaibab limestone

deposit, the most stable known underpinnings of the Earth's crust, and the reason for the settlement at the Uinkaret. A Launch Operations Center, the LOC, would control the activities of both facilities. These two locations were sufficiently south and close enough to the Earth's equator to take advantage of the velocity of the Earth's rotation. For eastward launches to the new world, even at the 36 degrees northern latitude of the Kaibab, it still meant 1,400km per hour velocity added to the launch generated velocity merely by the Earth's rotation. Five per cent of the low Earth orbit escape velocity would be gained by its proximity to the equatorial region.

But none of this would take place before heated debates were held in the engineering communities. Many thought it necessary to build the Great Migration Space Port in the peninsula, southwest of the Uinkaret, much closer to the equator and whose launch direction, east, took the flight paths over the eastern ocean waters. Launches from the Uinkaret's city proximity would have a disadvantaged rotational velocity of 300km per hour versus flights from the equatorial latitude. But it was impractical to build a launch facility so far from the city where the Earth's population had been centralized. Even in the middle of the Great Southern Peninsula, the velocity of the Earth's rotation would be 150km per hour less than the equatorial velocity of the Earth's rotation. Offsetting the penalty of the additional energy required to generate the shortfall of this rotational velocity difference was relatively insignificant compared to the total escape velocity to low Earth orbit of twenty-eight thousand km per hour. The efficiency gained by being able to recover the main engine first stage, which would fly back to the launch site after main engine cut-off, separation and jettison, easily offset the rotational velocity penalty, as well as the benefit of having all the technology of the Space Port in proximity to the Uinkaret, obviating the need to build any redundant infrastructure readily available at the city, but which was not available in the remote Peninsula. The main engine first stage would be returned to Earth while the craft parked in low Earth orbit, to wait until the second stage ignited for the escape from Earth orbit to Mars. The recovery and reuse of the main engine stages and booster rockets would be essential to the ability of the LOC's frequency of flight and cost/build efficiency for the thousands of flights required for the interplanetary migration. The Space Port would be built in the Uinkaret, not in the Great Southern Peninsula. Practical considerations outweighed the purely technical, slight, rotational velocity advantage, and construction of the Great Migration Port began.

The public commencement of the Autonomous Resettlement Kolony began in earnest after the Confederation meeting had taken place in the Great Hall. This would be the crowning achievement of one of a series of great projects undertaken since the lengthening of life discovery, the resettlement of the world's population to the Uinkaret, and then The Great Cataloging Activity of all life forms. The ARK project was the culmination of human development on Earth, ironically to sustain life independently on another planet. Konstantina Oblation's task would be to provide direction from the Office of Legal Ownership to the Confederation's Charter for the new world in matters relating to the initial colonization of Mars. Konstantina and her team would develop the ownership structure of the new society where of course, communal property laws would be administered initially by an officer corps charged with maintaining order and promoting the gradual development of the new independent colony.

Konstantina reminded herself that her role in society was a task of service, not engineering or production, all three the primary drivers of advanced societies. But she also realized that without the organizational control, without the civic structures by which human society functions and coexists in peaceful community, there could be no peaceful civil society. Man's relationship to man would descend to tribalism and the rule of the jungle – not of law, not strength of the intellect, nor of science and beauty.

V

And what of art and beauty?

The structures of the Uinkaret reflected the values of the new society. Architectural technology directed, that functional structures should be built with centuries, not decades of expected occupancy and civic use. Governmental advocacy demanded not only architectural brilliance, but public art in ways that contributed to the quality of life and acceptance of strictures of the new society. Population control and discipline was required of lives made ancient yet young. The inspiration for secular spiritual renewals spanning centuries was facilitated by public art and architecture that touched the lives of every citizen.

Shlater Curayan was recognized as the most accomplished and well-known artist of the Uinkaret, an eccentric but respected member of society. A brooding and pensive man, he did not attend Humboldt's speech at the Great Hall meeting. He did not care for social events in which he felt there was no political purpose of his attendance. Where he had no input to decisions and directions taken which were outside of the purview of his work. His visage matched his personality – dark, deep set eyes shadowed by the depth in which they set beneath his over-arching brow and full black eyebrows. Contrasting the pallid complexion of his high forehead, his dark thinning hair fell to one side, and when he was bent over something he was working on, it fell forward to obscure his face. His full black beard cut straight across his face, not above the height of his mustache, and was not connected to his very short sideburns. His entire lower face, fully one third of his head was entirely shadowed in the darkness of his beard and only a hint of his lips protruded from it. He was not a tall man, and was thickly built, yet there was a hint of agility and wiry strength in his movements, and his eyes pierced out from their darkness.

Though he considered the four colleagues, Humboldt, Konstantina, Alfrieda, and Rotfach part of his own circle of acquaintances and professional friends, he did not share their concern for the structures on the moon or the settlements on Mars, though he did share their enthusiasm for a social conscience. There had not yet been time nor expense for the luxury of art to be taken there. These were still highly engineered technological settlements where there was no place for things other than the engineered, purpose-built structures required for survival, and the legal and constitutional structures necessary for a civic society still within largely closed shelters. Art and beauty sponsored by society would come later. There would be no professional artists in the initial settlements of the new colonies. Any art or beauty produced there would be that which would be created out of a mature human need by the initial colonists once their basics for survival were provided, like ancient images painted on cave ceilings after a primitive hunt and the butchering and distribution of the meat, after the storage of roots and berries gathered for survival.

Curayan was disturbed by the lower rank assigned to artists in this highly technological society, where even an individual's increased lifespan was now dependent on the science of aging discovered as one of the results of DNA research. Although he had the relationship of one spousal assignment early in the second century of his life, he had not been paired with her until the age at which most people were beginning a relationship with their second spouse. At the age of one hundred thirty-four years, he had finally accepted a spousal partner, and he remained with this first partner for seventy-two years, by far many more years than any of his friends whose spousal assignments ranged from a normal thirty-four to fifty-seven years. Had the accident not happened that claimed her life, an accident that occurred while she was helping him erect a heavy sculptural commission, officially unauthorized and being installed in a public rural area rarely visited, he had intended to petition the authorities to enable him to continue a second spousal arrangement with the same woman, even after their unusually long first pairing. A highly unusual arrangement outside of the normal social conventions. Highly unusual and counterintuitive to modern society's desire to encourage limited length and multiple spousal assignments. It was a human engineered preference intended to enable continued emotional intensity, while also providing continued refreshing of the DNA code, so as not to allow a significant decrease in the rate of genetic diversification. Genetic control and editing were possible, but the scientific capability did not yet include the capacity to produce a male or female gamete and unite the germ cells. It was one thing to edit a multi-billion-unit DNA sequence. But to produce the two ladders of the double helix and control their recombination was still an act of nature alone. Though intellectually knowledgeable of the domestic civic sciences, he nonetheless resented the imposition of societal control over what he considered his private emotions. He resented the price that the length of lives required, yet was desirous to have as long a life as possible, to see his art evolve with his skills and experience, and to be able to fill the void which he perceived in a society so ruled by technology upon which its existence depended. And most of all now, he resented that the artist woman or man was not considered firstly essential in the establishment of the new Haven society of the fourth planet. He had always understood the lack of even the consideration of expenditure for art in the lunar and Mars colonies, established primarily for mineral extraction. But for the new society to be fully established on the fourth planet, he felt the inclusion of artists even more important. Essential for man's survival. Without which the expression of beauty, life itself would become a meaningless singularity of existence.

Shlater Curayan ascended the steps to the unauthorized dwelling which he and a few other colleagues had expropriated for their own uses, a temporary space not yet authorized for use. There were few undercurrents tolerated here at the population center, this being one of the very few temporarily unregistered, unofficial living spaces which Curayan had helped secure. It did not hurt that his influential friends like Humboldt and the others took his side, or perhaps more truly ignored this side of his behavior.

Hastily welded aluminum steps fashioned from scrap metal led the way upstairs. There were two fifth-story work spaces, separated by a partition of aluminum posts which supported the roof. Discarded rugs suspended on ropes between the posts divided the space into two nearly equal rooms. There was no power stairlift or elevator, and when he ascended the steps he was forced to sway from side to side like a sailor on a rolling ship, because the steps were not leveled plumb. But he was an artist first, he maintained, and although he was also a trained welder and carpenter who knew how to construct things out of wood or metal, the hastily constructed uneven steps helped him exit the world of social perfection from which he entered into the two rooms he had made into his own creative space.

Zabana heard him ascending the steps from the side of the space in which she worked. Also an artist trained in the tools of wood and metal sculpture, photography and painting, she was bent over a work table on which she was designing figures to be cut from nonferrous metals. Canvases were stacked beside her, and beside her lay half-completed sculptural forms. A bed made of blankets and pillows filled one corner for those days or nights when she chose not to return to her apartment. It was important not to leave the inspiration of a work not yet finished, to be able to bring it to a point where the emotion would not be lost, were its completion left to a later time.

She was a child compared to most of her colleagues, a young artist not yet at the century point of her life. Still, she was at an age where many had already had a spousal assignment and some had borne a child. Still, at the present time she had no interest in a spousal assignment, though in the many years to come she would be able to choose an assignment many times over again if the desire for a relationship or a child took hold of her. For now, she was interested in the intellectual curiosity with which she approached her work, and wanted to expend her emotions in the filling in of the spaces between the intellectual and the emotional in the context of her work. She was the youngest artist of the group of colleagues with whom she worked, and of all the others, male and female, none were at the present time eager for a child, or even for a spousal assignment out of which a child could be chosen. Some had already experienced a spousal assignment, and could easily have chosen her to become a new partner with whom to begin another assignment. But at the present time the answer for her was no, and Zabana found herself in the midst of a much older group, singular and independent, selfish for the necessary individuality to be able to create without the distraction of any unnecessary emotional entanglement or expenditure.

Shlater opened the door and called out for Zabana. She rose from her work table and embraced him in greeting. They were each other's mentor and most important critic. For him, she was the only woman or man to whom he could express emotion, long after his one tragic spousal assignment which had led, mostly by his own fault, to the great difficulty of his art and recovery from depression and despair. Among his most important acquaintances who were not part of the world of art were Humboldt, Alfrieda, Rotfach, and especially Konstantina. These all accepted this singular failure of his life, and while they chose to maintain and even strengthen the friendships which bound these four together, they extended their hands in friendship to Shlater, even though he kept himself apart at a distance. He considered the formality and not the emotion of his relationship to them.

As a young man, his skill, the dedication with which he approached his art, and the undeniable emotional content of his work – undeniable in a technologically oriented society which valued reason and logic above all others – brought recognition and success to him early in his ascendant career. And over time, even the perceived difficulties of his relationship with Zabana had been reconciled. Eighty-seven-year-old Zabana Oblation's relationship with the two hundred eighty-six-year-old Shlater Curayan was finally accepted without prejudice by Konstantina, the mother of Zabana, her only child.

There were no windows on her side of the work space, on this side the room where Zabana worked. It was set against the wall of the building against which it was constructed. One skylight illuminated the space and provided natural light during the day. On the other side where Shlater worked were two crude clerestory windows set high on the wall, one looking out north towards the rim of the canyon, and one facing east. His side, too, was illuminated during the day by an additional skylight in the ceiling. Only a partial partition of rugs was fastened to the aluminum support posts separating both sides, not all the way to the ceiling, so that light from the clerestories also filtered into the opposite side where Zabana worked and were visible from her side of the space. Both skylights on either side of the partitioned room were crudely fashioned from salvaged materials. If the infrequent rains were accompanied by winds from a certain direction, containers were set on the floor beneath them to catch any leaking water. It was the price of independence in a non-sanctioned workspace, redolent of artists of antiquity. He set two packages down on the corner of Zabana's work table, removed his coat and threw it onto the floor in front of the door.

"Something to eat and drink," he said, as if preoccupied with other thoughts.

"Let's take them into the other room."

"What are you working on?"

She closed the light that illuminated the surface of her table, and moved aside the imaging surface of the magnification instrument with which she used as she formed and modeled tiny sculptural pieces. Some were images of plants, animals, wings of birds, beaks, the claws of a foot or a feather. Her tiny human sculptures may have been the arms or legs of a dancer suspended on a wire around which they were movable, rotatable with the push of a finger or a gentle breath. A hand, a face, in portrait or in profile. A triangle of female sexuality, a cupped breast or fingers etched on the surface of a miniature scrotum, phalli like hanging sausages. Zabana's work was intimate, interior, modest, bold, introverted, extroverted, sexual, chaste, delicate, vulnerable, strong, demanding, articulate, accurate, whimsical. It was everything she was.

Curayan picked up the packages that he had set on the corner of her table and took them into the other room. In the corner of the room beneath the east window was a low table, with two zabutons arranged beside it, next to each other on corners of the table so that both could see out the window. The artist's work was scattered about the room, in finished and unfinished states. The floor had not been swept, and was littered with the detritus of his work and of living in this space. One of the packages contained two containers of hot tea. The other package – cheeses, meats, and a narrow loaf of bread. A few small pieces of dried fruit. He arranged them on the table and waited for Zabana to finish her work. He brushed aside anything that had been left on the pillows.

Shlater Curayan was a draftsman, a painter, and a sculptor, but in this space, though he might plan a sculptural commission here, that work was left to his studio in the artists foundry provided by the Confederation. Here he pursued his private work, paintings large and small, things not sanctioned, private, an outlet for his creativity which enabled him to express more intimately that which he created more fully in his public works.

Zabana was not the daughter of an ancient patriarch whose duty it was to bring forth a child to continue a lineage. Genetic engineering had made the vitality of their lives equal. Age was not overcome by youth. The present was the historical opposite. There was freedom to choose love now which lasted centuries and was not limited to only a few decades of life. There was power in this new equation which was not ransomed and held by briefest time.

The moon was rising in the sky beyond the horizon, as Zabana and Shlater knelt onto the cushions. Rising in the east, it was preceded by the blue-green star to the left above it that had already crested the horizon. Mars, where art ought also to be, thought Curayan, a necessity of the new Confederation, before it briefly dimmed as the moon also broke above the mountains and the canyons of the horizon. The moon was ascending, soon it would be out of view from the east facing window. Now it cast its reflected glow against the glass of the skylights, so that were the lights in their work space extinguished it would have been capable of casting its penumbra upon the floor.

"It will not be a true haven without art," Shlater spoke in the silent room. And Zabana, with the perpetual hue of an island sun in her skin, silently vowed to will herself to the new planet despite the Confederation's perceived lack of necessity of art.

"I will bring my color like the trunks of trees to the new world, a stabilizing force like a green forest with the blue sky above," she thought.

"I shall not leave behind the genes of the indigenous race from which my mother chose me to spring forth. I shall emerge again on the shores of a new land, not consumed by a new race of settlers, but taking vital part," she continued in thought to herself alone. She was as slender and tall as her mother, a bronze-olive complexion and dark eyes, raven black hair, and an open, large-eyed face, pale lips; but with a gentleness strong enough to hold your gaze. From fine gold loop earrings, small figures were suspended which danced when she moved her head or shook with laughter. Her limbs were well-muscled but not muscular, her body and movements entirely feminine, and though her hair was very dark, there was no coarseness to it, cascading about her face in its fineness when she moved, despite being brushed back away from her forehead. She had secured it in a top knot in order to concentrate on her work.

Shlater still saw something in her expression which he had seen from the moment they had first met. It was not his to hold, but something to perceive. It was not a need nor a request, but something that was. Something in her eyes like the description of those of a newborn child by a friend, a new parent, who said that when he gazed into the eyes of his first-born child, he felt he was looking into infinity, the black pupils like a night sky into which he was falling. An infant's eyes not yet turned as blue as the blue of the sky.

Returning to the table from their thoughts they began to eat. The distance of years between them no longer made a difference in this world of lengthened lives. Later, the table would be cleared, Shlater would tidy up this corner space, and Zabana would return to her side of the studio, open the light and return to her work. Shlater would descend the steps to walk for a few minutes in the ascending moonlight of the evening before he too, returned to mount the stairway to their studio and work. Still later, they would mix the eternal infinity together. The giving and getting of life. They held each other apart but yet together for only the briefest moment before they slept, before the blue-green planet waned and descended from the sky unseen, pulling the moon behind it.

vi

The lengthening of lives had presented complex issues relating to private versus public ownership. All of the issues of human development on Earth had been experienced during the millenniums of man's development. It was not something that was dropped into place overnight: these had evolved and survived through countless wars, famines, pestilences, and various form of rule, cruelty, and suffering. And through especially the modern centuries of the past one or two millenniums, various forms of public and private ownership had evolved along with the failures and successes of succeeding governmental administrations. But this time, for the new planet, it was different. For the time being there could be no private ownership, no private self-serving initiative on Mars. All of the operations there at the permanent outpost on the plains surrounding Aeolis Mons would be, by necessity, public. There would be private companies contracted by the government to train and equip specifically skilled individuals who would provide goods and services to the colony, but these were all governmental controlled activities. There could be no independent private activity in that new world. All would be "publicly" owned by the Confederation government, for it would be a totally new world where none in society of any kind had existed before. Now however, there would be the creation of a more complete and complex society, not a mirror image of the human condition on Earth, but a structure and geography appropriate to the new world, with conditions and requirements that would differ.

Once established with the ten thousand flights from Earth, there would be a scheduled transition from public only property rights, to those private property rights appropriate for specific conditions. There would need to be a recognition of the efforts and results with the incentive of private ownership enabled by the public laws of the confederation and the future constitutional framework of the new world. But these activities would be left to the perhaps distant future. Much public, collective activity would have to take place before privatization discussions would be appropriate.

Independence presented interesting conundrums. This was a new world not accessible to those responsible for its creation. Individuals like Konstantina or Humboldt, Alfrieda or Rotfach, and at this point certainly not the artists Shlater or Zabana – none of these would be among those chosen to travel to the planet which would initially be constructed and organized under their supervision from Earth. Journeys to the planet would be one-way transits for the resettlement population. Even now with the permanent mining and technological research facilities on Mars, there was a significant length of assignment required before workers were returned to Earth. An agreement to a permanent assignment on Mars was even more highly compensated. But it had taken a certain kind of engineer to agree to a compensation that would either be returned to Earth, not for his or her own benefit, but for the benefit of those left behind, or for the promise of a future remuneration after centuries of development, when there might be something on Mars to buy or invest in, and something to pay with. But there was no possibility for return trips to Earth for the ARK colonists. Any resources or energy expended on the development of Mars would remain on the planet for the benefit of ARK. Even communication with Earth from Mars became complex, when the time for signal transepts ranged from a matter of four minutes with the planet in opposition, to over twenty minutes of signal delay when the planets were at conjunction. Dialogue is extremely difficult and time consuming, and from a practical standpoint impossible, when each response from the other planet requires between four and twenty minutes of signal travel time across interplanetary space. These kinds of communications between planets required a disciplined approach even for scheduled signal transmissions, an even more complex protocol in times of emergency. There would be no resources for the absolutely unnecessary.

A framework constitution would need to be developed to take the new world from an exploratory outpost to a fully functioning society. There would need to be a progression from governmental ownership and control of geographic colonization, and the turnover to private individuals for the eventual balancing of public versus private ownership. A process that could take generational centuries in an unfolding with requirements which could not be fully imagined.

Public utilities and infrastructure, legal and political systems, monetary systems, terrestrial communication, agriculture, industrial production, environmental controls, energy production, and eventually art and entertainment – all these and more would be developed to be apportioned out in a combination of public and private ownership.

A task so complex and time consuming, it could only be left to the chance of seemingly random events met by the initiative of human ingenuity, controlled only by agreement within the framework of processes outlined in a new Constitution.

No one could actually know how it would work. No one could anticipate nor imagine the details of a future Mars.

A new world not to be witnessed or experienced by the old world, except through transmissions of video and data across the unfeeling emptiness of dispassionate interplanetary space.

The commencement of the Autonomous Resettlement Kolony project was to begin in earnest. The Great Cataloging Activity of Earth life DNA was complete. Nine of the genetic records of life on Earth would fly to the ARK on Mars, and one placed in a solar orbit – a final scapegoat TGCA repository rocketed to an interplanetary, near absolute zero, exile around the sun. Covenants of Earth life to be carried to the ARK and beyond.

Ten thousand flights, ten million kilograms. Twenty thousand citizens, each one with a limiting baggage weight of a hundred kilograms including all personal possessions, required two thousand of the ten thousand flights for this human cargo of two million kilograms, leaving just eight million kilograms of materials transported by eight thousand flights with which to construct a new world. In addition to the people and supplies brought on these flights would be the materials salvaged from the remains of the ships themselves, the ejected heat shields, fabrics and cords of descent parachutes, metals of the re-entry vehicles and the vehicles themselves, engines, motors, structures, remaining propellants, wires, electronics, tools, and interior furnishings. All would be available for the essential recycling of all spacecraft flight materials in addition to specific items planned to be transported to the new planet – all materials would be recycled and eventually, when the flights to the new world ended, there would even be desperate attempts to find the materials which were lost during re-entry to the new world. Nothing would be, nothing could be wasted. And so many imagined unknowns to those who surmised them in silence. The recycling of the ships themselves, and of each particle and gram of material transported from Earth and scratched from the surface of the new Haven would not be an optional activity. It would prove to be not only a requirement, it would become a necessity for survival, and one not sufficient for the task, absent human ingenuity and the will to survive.

During the period of Earth's history in which we had struggled, survived, and developed in the ten thousand years of our human story we had come to this moment. During the Cretaceous-Tertiary extinction event, sixty million years earlier, all exposed organisms were killed and the entire terrestrial biosphere had nearly perished. Non-avian dinosaurs and three quarters of all species were lost. The mammals, birds, amphibians, crocodilians, turtles, and lepidosaurs that survived, were not to be buried and burned to extinction within the layer of iridium containing sediment that blanketed the Earth. Iridium, an element abundant in the asteroids and comets that had torn through the Earth's atmosphere and impacted ocean and land. Over these sixty million years after the K-Pg event – an event which released an energy equivalent to one hundred teratons of TNT – the species that survived evolved into their modern forms. The survival of life, the continuum of individually delicate strings of DNA with their billions of genetic markers that had survived the burning, and then also survived the ebb and flow of repeated frozen glaciations. Throughout all of which our ancestors prevailed and eventually unlocked the code of life to preserve the ability to survive again, by capturing and preserving the record of life in the archives of the TGCA. The capability to survive, to withstand a natural calamity so vast that survival could not be assured in any one specific place. This was the premise and now the knowledge and sure forecast of what Humboldt Noraxton had spoken about to the gathered assembly at the Great Hall of Quaternary Plaza. The Confederation would assure the continuation of the human species undeterred by the potential physical destruction of one world, with the Haven of a second to assure human survival, and preserve the DNA evolved over the past sixty million years. In five billion years, the exhaustion of the hydrogen of our own star will cause the destruction of both Earth and Mars worlds, but by then it could be assumed that a far greater technology will have evolved to enable the survival from this much greater challenge. That is, if man learned again the capacity to survive, greater than the capacity to destroy, a bitter lesson to have been learned in the past ten thousand years of our recorded human history. We would hope that it would not have to be learned again on Mars, the new Haven, and that if it had to be relearned, we could yet overcome it once more. For Noraxton and the leaders of the Confederation, it was this hope, and for his friends the task, to organize and plan the actual sequence of events to help to bring it all about.

Ten thousand flights, and the chosen people transported to the fourth planet. Ten thousand ships to assemble and outfit for the journey. Uncertain lifeboats with no chance of return. A Fifty-Year Plan, to provide support brought to the fourth blue orb from the third blue planet Earth in order to secure the first two generations in Haven. A seed planted for a harvest, the grain of which the planters will not reap. The interplanetary settlers will separate the seed from the chaff to elicit the will to survive, prosper, and prevail from across the blackness and cold of space which curves and stretches between conjunction and opposition and forbiddingly lies between these two blue orbs, the third and fourth planets circling our sun.

Before he made preparations to end this one of many long days, Rotfach Theoretrics turned once more to his work screens and sent instructions to his engineering team and the technical leaders of the various project sub-teams. He would travel to the construction site of the Space Port taking form even as the first cargo flights were able to journey towards the fourth blue planet. He wanted to see with his own eyes the progress and physical layout of the site where building had already begun. A point in the surrounding hills, already designated as a public viewing promontory once the Port was finished, is where he would first stop, to see an overview of the project which would be the finest and most noble construct of his centuries long career, and one in which he hoped, without reason, that he himself could escape the bonds of Earth's gravity and become an argonaut on a journey to see the new world to which his effort was dedicated, Project ARK.

The existing space port would proceed to launch cargo flights using the facilities supporting the permanent Mars mining and technology colony, while some of the new space port and launch pads were still in the form of architectural drawings. The number and location of the launch pads had already been determined, surveyed, and the contours of grading and other ground preparations could be seen from the location of the future observation facility on which he stood now, the morning after the Great Hall proclamation.

The two launch facilities, one for cargo and one for manned flights, had already been excavated and the first RMLF – Robotic Mission Launch Facility – pad was already operational and ready to launch its first robotic cargo ship. This launch facility for unmanned vehicles would be expanded to include eight launch pads, fanning out from the central launch operations and control center which would serve both human and robotic cargo launches.

The second complex, whose footprint was only beginning to take shape in the dry ground of the desert, would be the Human Spaceflight Launch Facility. The HSLF would have fewer pads extending out from the launch control facility than the RMLF. Its pads would have to support only one fourth as many launches as cargo flights, but still it needed at least three pads, one of which would always be available in the event of a catastrophic failure.

This entire new space port was in addition to the facility which now supported the permanent Mars colony. This existing facility would continue normal operations as the ARK project began to be implemented. The ARK project with its many thousands of planned flights required that the new dedicated Port to be designed with a capability robust enough to sustain the vastly higher quantities of launches. Once the new RMLF and HSLF were completed and in use, the existing flight complex now serving the first Mars colony, would remain operational and redundant to serve unforeseen difficulties and challenges.

In a few minutes Rotfach descended to the site level, to speak directly with the architects, designers, surveyors, and tradesmen who were working on ARK. Well aware of risks for projects that must use concurrent engineering, he wanted to stay as close as possible to the men and women who would build out this facility. To them he would owe a debt of gratitude for their ability to take the drawings, numbers, calculations of his project

teams and turn them into the tangible Space Port facility that
was beginning to take form in front of him. He knew that with
large concurrent engineering projects it should be anticipated
that the execution teams, at their best, would anticipate
problems and recommend alternatives. All while moving
forward with the construction of the port.

vii

The permanent engineering and mining settlement on the
planet Mars was situated on the shore of the Great Southern
Sea, at the southern edge of Iapygia quadrangle MC-21, in the
temperate zone above the equator. Here the northern highlands
fall away to the edge of the sea, and eventually follow the great
Mawrth Vallis trench to the towering depths of the great ocean
that spanned three fourths of the southern hemisphere. The
sliding tectonic plates beneath the shore of this great sea had
exposed areas where surface mining was possible for the
minerals which had been scraped, crushed, pushed up and out,
from beneath the plates as they bowed, buckled, and slid under
one another over the eons, and then backfilled with water and
the inevitable life of the seas and then the lands. But no land
animals were found by the first exploratory teams, and no fishes
in the sea. Plant life covered the land masses, and plankton and
diatomic creatures filled the seas, in a symbiotic relationship
not yet understood compared to the plant, animal, and aquatic
life on Earth. And in spite of the absence of fishes and other sea
creatures, the atmosphere proved suitable for man.

Weaker gravity made heavy work possible for the men and
women and the machines with which they had begun to explore
and utilize the new world. Using only carbon fiber robotic
exoskeletons, some of the work which formerly required the
use of heavy machinery, could be done safely by individual
men and women. From this area of the original permanent
mining post, all the way east to the great collapsed volcanic
cone and fresh water inland sea with the Aeolis Mon within its
midst, the scope and breadth of the colony had begun to

establish itself on the northern plains. Meanwhile the Great Southern Sea, covering most of the southern hemisphere, remained largely unknown and unexplored by the engineering teams which had established the first permanent colony on the planet.

The men and women of the original Mars mining colony had been sent on assignment commitments lasting six Earth years. The first-year journey to the planet, four Earth years on the planet, and the sixth-year return to Earth. The long journey to the planet and the return required too much time and too much resources to enable shorter assignments. And some of the explorer-engineers re-signed for a second or third contract, essentially never intending to return to Earth until a significant period of their lives had been expended on the fourth blue orb. Were they eventually to return, significant muscular skeletal changes occurred after such extended periods of one-third gravity on the Martian surface, and then an almost one year journey of weightlessness during the return to Earth. The adaptation to weightlessness during the sixth-year return journey was not as stressful as the initial flight to Mars, having transitioned from less than Earth's gravity to weightlessness. But the return to Earth gravity after six years caused grave adaptation difficulties. Severe adaptation difficulties were experienced by those who had completed multiple Mars assignments.

The six-year commitment made by each of the mining colonists, required not only exceptional intelligence and mental stability, but an overriding physical strength. An initially pleasant sensation was the result of the reduced gravitational stress on their bodies, and over time their bodily systems adapted to the new atmosphere composed with different percentages of oxygen, carbon dioxide, and nitrogen than the Earth's atmosphere. After four years on Mars, the adaptation to lower gravity was complete. Then the return to Earth required the reverse effort of adaptation to higher gravity resulting in endoskeletal and soft tissue distress, and the need to acclimatize to the different atmospheric gas concentrations.

Due to its 1.9 Earth-year solar orbit, and an almost equal tilt on axis, 25 degrees versus the Earth's 23.5, Mars possesses seasons similar to Earth but almost double in length. The length of each day is near to those of Earth days – 24 hours and 40 minutes. The circadian rhythm of an individual adapts very quickly to the similar length of a Martian sol. The four-year on-planet assignment commitment fit very well with the seasons and mission length. In four Earth years, each scientist/engineer would experience two full cycles of Martian years, each Martian year being equal to 687 Earth days.

Project Haven's ARK, the Advanced Resettlement Kolony, would proceed and expand from the engineering mission already established on the Northern Hemisphere Highlands above the location of the Great Marineris Sea Trench. This great rift beneath the Great Southern Sea extends from Phoenicis Lacus west, to the Margritifer Sinus quadrangle east. The new Haven colony would be established farther east to where the Great Inland Sea of Aeolis lay, amidst which the extinct volcanic cone rises within the center of the 150kilometer diameter freshwater inland sea, the pure source of life for the inhabitants of ARK. The great plains of Aeolis south of the equator would be the site of the new society, while the mining and engineering facility would remain west and in the northern hemisphere, the site of valuable ore and minerals which would be shipped east to Haven through a series of inland canals and barrier islands along the northern shore of the Great Southern Sea.

viii

Rotfach watched and felt the vibrations at his feet and the roar of the machines at work on the space port worksite. He closed his eyes and thought of his colleagues and friends – Humboldt, with his burden of decision, and the possibility and dread of recognition of the end – Alfrieda, with her concerns of environmental disengagement and technology that was capable of replacing what was once human to touch and feel –

Konstantina, whose debate arguments between themselves defined the legal precepts required for a society to exist, versus the preeminent value of technology with which he himself advocated.

In the distance, an ARK cargo ship was readying to launch at the existing mining colony space port. Now Rotfach imagined and watched with his mind, feeling the power and impulses transmitted through the air as the spacecraft fired its engines and began its ascent. He could hear and feel the arc of its trajectory as its gyros moved the nose cone to the east to lay it over to begin its flight to orbit. He imagined and felt the concussion of the first stage separation from the craft after main engine cut-off, the concussion of the pyrotechnic bolt cutters which released the upper stage, the payload stacked on top of it, ready to surge forward. The second stage engine was primed for the ignition burn of the unsymmetrical dimethyl hydrazine, pressurized and mixed with the equally pressurized flow of dinitrogen tetroxide which entered the combustion chamber of the rocket engine. There is no stopping the combustion of this 2nd stage rocket fuel. It will spontaneously ignite, and once ignited it will burn until exhausted.

Opening his eyes, he imagined and could see the effect of the spreading contrail of the 1st stage combustion which formed a billowing linear cloud rising into the sky, the flames of the second stage rocket engine no longer visible to his naked eye as it arced east beyond eyesight. He pondered the human combustion within himself, enabled by catalytic chemistry at the molecular level within his human cells, and the cells of every living creature on Earth, and in the cellular life of every living thing which had also been discovered in Haven.

With a weary pride and no fear of the future, he looked out over the Uinkaret plains, and the recent excavations for the Space Ports. He would play his part, and the parts of his friends and colleagues would also play out, determined to establish a new world, a second chance if required, an optimistic Confederation hopeful that it would endure together for ages to come, the sister planets Earth and Mars. But if life on mother

Earth were to be lost, the new world would survive and perhaps humankind would rise again on the second human world. Momentarily he felt a great age upon himself, though he had seen only three hundred seventy-eight years, merely one third of a possible life. But it was a momentary pause which passed quickly, and as he descended from the viewing promontory, his youthful energy returned, and he set about to his tasks at the burgeoning space port. There was no time to lose. They were chasing survival for an eternity of being.

The first stage rockets were returning to the launch site as he continued his observation. The powerful rocket motors of the returning first booster stages, which had just launched the robotic cargo craft towards near Earth orbit in which to cruise in a weightless orbit until the second stage fired, now reignite their engines as they approached the same multiple launch pad complex from which they had arisen. There was a pattern of return platforms surrounding the central launch pad, one for each of the three booster cores which had been attached to the central rocket motor which lifted the first stage to MaxQ. Like a delicate ballet, they reignited as they approached the launch complex, spread their landing legs returning gently to their assigned spaces, and finally, settling on the return platforms, the engines shut down, the roar of their thrust subsided, and they stood like spent titans, bruised and scarred, ready to guard the central booster core as they awaited its return, the last to settle upon the central return platform. Already the refurbishment teams for the next flight began their work, as the men and women assigned to this task moved to the launch return platforms. Preparations for the next of the eight thousand cargo flights which would supply the new world of Haven had already begun in earnest. Haven would not wait. ARK had commenced, and the ships had begun to fly.

We have started on our journey, thought Rotfach, now transitioning himself to the work of the day. It is good work, to ensure the survival of our world in the next. A testament to man's ingenuity and understanding of his small place in the innumerable stars of the present universe. Always reminding himself that the work here must not only be imagined, it must be fulfilled, and if not completed, could our work ever be complete, it must still proceed apace. We must not turn back – move forward, don't delay, except for what is required to be delayed to be human. Press forward with confidence and the inevitability which brought our genetic code forward from the first universal ancestor, three and a half billions of years ago. That was mere hundreds of millions of years after the creation itself of what had become the third and fourth blue orbs – Earth and Mars – coalesced from the dust clouds of stars, a part of one of countless universes which will all eventually vanish into one across a singularity and blackness, with a hope to burst forth once again, to repeat this thirty-five-billion-year cycle again and again, and unendingly again in the infinite, unmeasurable, and unending, space and time.

ix

Shlater and Zabana awakened and made a small breakfast of the remains of their simple dinner of the night before, then descended the uneven steps from their studio to the city below. Work called them to the commissions they had been contracted to complete at the double inverted pyramids of the Great Hall of the renamed "Interplanetary" Confederation, where Humboldt had addressed the assembled dignitaries and guests the evening before. They were part of an atelier of artists assigned to produce a series of panels depicting the history of the Confederation and the assemblage of Earth's life at the Uinkaret. Over the millenniums of humankind's development – scientific, political, and moral – there never ceased the need to express the imagination, creativity, and truth-telling of the artist. Though present-day life was dependent on the technology of the modern society without which man could not wish to survive, there never ceased the need to create and participate in, even if only in the enjoyment of, the consumption of art and various expressions of art. It was evident in the beauty of the most modern, functional, and technologically sophisticated architecture of the Uinkaret. Without the aspect of function and beauty, no architecture would be considered great. Beauty was evident also in the design of the most modest or pedestrian signage placed throughout the Uinkaret. With the level of society and technology upon which it depended, there also followed an increasing dependency on the value and beauty of the arts which was supported by the wealth of the ascendant society by which humankind had elevated its existence, as if the lengthening of lives followed by necessity the need to retain and utilize the joy of life to which the modern world had acceded, and learned finally through peaceful means, to create a kind of Kingdom of Haven on Earth. For many generations now, war remained a distant memory, a shameful recollection of brutal, immoral, dishonest, human behavior that had not yet been wrung out of man's coarser proclivities, though now it was to be a genetically modified proclivity, of necessity.

Meeting with their colleagues at the Social Containment Complex, Shlater and Zabana entered the Plex's Flaxen Cafe. They were an unusual couple in that neither wanted to utilize the Club facilities for sexual therapy, though it was almost unheard of that couples remained monogamous without at least an occasional therapy session, especially for the female of the parings. It was one of the guiltless activities that had evolved over the millenniums when war disappeared. But at least for now they felt no need between the two of them for therapy outside their own fulfilling relationship. Even though Shlater, many years her senior, felt that Zabana should eventually come to realize the benefits of at least an occasional therapeutic STA session.

Taking part of the regularly scheduled meetings at the Plex, the board members of the artist association had not yet been able to see to the completion of the themes and specific topics to be depicted in of all the panels of the frescoes which were to cover the interior walls of the hallways leading to the chamber of the inverted pyramids at the Confederation Hall. The thematic execution of the murals was to be determined by the artists themselves, and only communicated as a courtesy to the governing members of the Confederation who had been given only the outline of the thematic portrayals. The interpretations of the murals were to be chosen by the artists themselves in their license to create as bold a work as the architecture in which it would be contained. Final responsibility for the content was held by the senior members of the artists association, not the Confederation, who were, though generally older and most experienced, still the boldest and most avant-garde members of the arts community. Their judgments and interests pushed boundaries in service of beauty and emotional content, impacting the viewers sensibilities to the furthest extent possible to inspire, awaken, and remind those most learned and serious members of the Confederation who passed through these halls, of their humanity on their way to the great chamber and their societal deliberations.

Shlater was one of the artist elders, whose responsibility for content he accepted with gratitude that his work had allowed him this honor. His status accorded himself as much flexibility for control as possible. And Zabana, still centuries younger than him, inspired him as he knew she too would be elevated by the truth of her own work and judgement in the centuries to come. Not that he could know the future that would be his or hers.

On their way to the Plex, a cargo rocket rose from the Space Port launch complex, the same that Rotfach witnessed from that desert construction site. They saw the contrails of its arc as it sped, now nearly horizontal to their view, to the eastern horizon, MECO, and then low Earth orbit. Now, out of sight and in orbit on the other side of the world, reignition and a second stage burn sent the spacecraft from this world to the next.

x

Preliminary calculations of the requirements for the human flights determined that for the eight to twelve-month journey, only ten people could be aboard a spacecraft, with an average body weight limitation of seventy-five kilograms and one-hundred kilograms personal items per voyager, calculating an average limitation based on six men and four women. Later flights, when the colonist population reached at least ten thousand, children would be considered with a passenger's mix of four men, four women, and four children per flight. A total of twenty thousand colonists needed to be transported in the two thousand planned human flights. But there was no spacecraft yet flown which had a capacity of ten aboard and provisions enough for an interplanetary journey. The men now living and working at the engineering and mining complex had never traveled with more than five aboard on spacecrafts outfitted for industrial purposes. Never before had the Confederation spacecraft ferried civilian human cargo unaccustomed to the rigors of less comfortable provisions than those experienced with terrestrial travel.

Konstantina Oblation knew that the addition of children to the later flights, after the initial colonists had established suitable conditions, was considered a necessary complication. The genetic selection available on Earth, with the obviation of disease and the selection of the extended life genetic therapy would not be available in the new planet until the level of the pioneering colony could support such technological and medical requirements independently. It was not possible that children would be born on Mars until the genetic engineering and control was in place. This required that the development of the medical facilities for genetic obstetrics in the new society be commenced immediately. And the development of the infrastructure that children required – schools, day care, pediatrics and most importantly, the time and effort required to raise children – was in opposition to the effort put forward in the initial creation of the new society itself – the work that the pioneering men and women undertook to infrastructure a new planet.

From her conference room at the Office of Legal Ownership Konstantina convened a morning meeting. The lawyers present had all attended the meeting of the Confederation the previous evening, and were still processing the speech that Humboldt Noraxton had given. There was much talk and conversation as the legal minds poured cups of hot liquid, essential coffee, and formed into groups for small talk of varying intensity and subject. Gradually, refreshed and stimulated by the caffeine, they made their way to their seats at the conference table. Before all were settled, Konstantina, impatient most with herself, began the meeting.

"Now we have officially begun the human quest to explore and propagate humankind beyond our own planet," as Humboldt had proclaimed in his own words, "in the advancement of a new society to be fully formed in the vicinity of our Martian outpost. Optimally, two independent societies in a symbiotic relationship are what we strive for."

"The old world will build the new world which in due time must become an equal, fully functional society, where opportunity equals or exceeds every facet of our present-day existence here on Earth. It is what we must strive to achieve, and we must accept no less."

By the time these words had been heard by her colleagues around the table, sobering thoughts settled into the minds of each who took their seat. And their comments began to flow over the surface of the table which separated them, monitored and transcribed and appearing already archived on holographic screens as they spoke, which appeared in front of each of the attendees.

"We must structure the social and legal precepts of Haven, initially with our oversight, in order to benefit the new society using the experience of what we have achieved here at the Uinkaret."

"All of us must surely agree that what we have learned, from our own difficulties which we faced as we made our own new society here during the consolidation of other settlements which were far-flung across our planet, must be used to help establish our Martian colonists. We must revisit with an understanding of what took place as we faced those same difficulties and complexities which arose with the introduction of the lengthening of lives technology here on Earth, and what it might or might not mean for Haven."

"We need to anticipate and plan for in vitro intervention, and even the alternate certainty of natural birth in the new environment which will become necessary if there is a delay of in vitro implementation, and the ramifications of such unaltered genetic profiles of children born to their genetically altered parents who were transported from Earth."

"How quickly will technology be made available for controlled succession and birth? Will lengthened lives be immediately possible, or must it be delayed pending the ability to achieve the acquisition of a delayed technological capability?"

"What does this mean for those who must coexist with individuals who have one century of life expectancy vs ten, when some of the children born with the enhanced life gene will outlive a natural parent by centuries?"

"These are questions we have faced before, unprepared, and having to learn as we lived and adapted to the challenges and requirements of a new order which has become our natural order now. But history can recite the chaos and confusion that we had to recognize and pre-conceptualize in order to move forward with human feelings, needs, and societal responsibilities, which led ultimately to our own Quaternary Uinkaret."

"The new long-lived colonists on Mars, the first twenty thousand must be able to mentor and pass on the knowledge and technology with which they brought to Haven from Earth. It is up to us to help them, and give them the structured planning with flexible options on how to implement their new society. It will not be a one generational task. It has taken us ten millenniums to have arrived to this place where we are sitting at now. Surely we must afford them the centuries of a plan."

"These are difficult questions which must be considered and entered into the complicated linear equations which we have postulated into the planning for variant possibilities."

And, so on and on it went, a compendium of initial thoughts captured and combined into a holographic data summary which would be pruned and preened to anticipate, control, and allow human life the freedom to live, and to survive in a new world. With assistance and support from the old world until it may no longer exist, and to continue to be able to provide support and guidance, resources and technology, by the prescriptions left behind after the possibility that it would be gone. A sobering thought. All here in the now and present needed to plan for a new future to begin. None of the living now may still exist to see it beyond the present. They will surely never travel to the place that will become the future.

None present, would ever be able to survive, to live, and to work in Haven.

xi

Humboldt Noraxton slept soundly for only part of the night, after his speech at the Confederation Hall. He had been received most kindly even though the message of his speech was difficult. In reality he announced the possible end of the world as it was known, within a span of time so short that it might have been cause for a general panic which he now knew would not occur.

But he had awakened fitfully, without a feeling of having been sufficiently rested, and he arose from his bed slowly.

"Perhaps there is too much blind hope in the technology that has transformed our own known world," he said to no one other than himself, as a coffee presented itself to him even as he had not yet extended his outstretched hand to receive it from the dispensing machine. In fact, the Director- Population Control did not think to describe the flights to Mars as anything other than ten thousand lifeboat flights. A tragic thought to think of losing all that surrounded those privileged to live in the Uinkaret metropolis, as he looked out over the city from the view afforded his flat. He dressed, readied himself for work, decided that he would use another sexual chit at the club in the afternoon, and afterwards soon found himself reviewing the screens in his office, to which he had been alerted holographically before he had even left his home. The warning was clear. The trouble was, no one could know if it was a warning or a harbinger. Was it simply a statement of fact about something that would surely happen at some unidentified and unknowable time, in the near or the distant far future? Was it in the spirit of an archaic evocation that could merely mean the search for a new home? Or was it something as simple as a desire for change? It was Humboldt's hope that both human worlds – one which existed and one which was only planned – would survive to live together, joined by the ten-minute communication delay of the interplanetary signals that went constantly back and forth between the planets at the speed of light.

"It is very odd," Humboldt thought to himself. "Will we ever be able to accept the fact of this communications delay between Uinkaret and Haven. History records in millenniums past, that letters between distant communicants could take months to be sent and received. Between our two worlds there will be mere minutes between messages sent and received. Will man now ever be able to accept the grace of patience in world accustomed to instant gratification?"

xii

Human cargo required a shuttle vehicle, not the standard rocket of a cargo ship or of a spacecraft carrying a few men and women to the permanent mining mission. It would not be able to plummet and parachute to the surface, it would have to be able to survive reentry and fly to the surface. The hold of this ship would also need to be able to become a building block of permanent structures, a modular construction structure capable of being deconstructed and reused at the new Mars settlement. Nothing would be wasted of the precious kilograms that were brought to the planet's surface across interplanetary space.

The engineering teams had processed and evaluated sufficient test launches to know that modular booster cores could be added to the 1st stage launch vehicles to provide the lift capability required for the heavier human shuttle vehicles. 2nd stage rockets which would send the shuttles from low Earth orbit to the transit to Mars would require longer burn times, but fuel loads could be increased for the additional thrust time required. These 2nd stage interplanetary booster vehicles would remain attached to the shuttles and provide power and rotational stability for the journey into Mars orbit. The 2nd stage rocket engines would be separated from the shuttle vehicles to deorbit and land independently on the surface of Mars in order to be recycled and used for equipment, building materials, and power generation, much as the 1st stage launch vehicles returned to launch pads on Earth to be recycled there.

A shuttle craft would have to descend to the surface after an incandescent reentry through the Martin atmosphere, the density of which was less than Earth's, especially at higher altitudes aloft, though with its different concentrations of nitrogen, carbon dioxide, and oxygen, versus the concentrations in the Earth's atmosphere. The higher oxygen concentration, approximately 25% near the equatorial plains of the colonist's destination was offset by a decrease in the concentration of nitrogen to 74%. Given the heavier weight of diatomic oxygen, at 32g/mol versus nitrogen at 28g/mol, the density of the atmosphere at the surface was still significantly less than the surface density of the Earth's atmosphere at sea level, due to the one third less gravity for the less massive planet. Drag chutes and extreme wing flap designs would be required to lower the landing speed to acceptable limits as the shuttles landed on runways which would have to be lengthened considerably versus an equivalent runway on planet Earth.

xiii

When Alfrieda Praxis arose the next day after Humboldt's speech, tears had begun to moisten her eyes and they remained closed to the morning as she awakened from a dream in which she climbed the steep path up one of the foothills of the mountains which rose north of the Uinkaret, below the tree line altitude of the distant summits. Reaching the top, climbing over the surface roots of trees which had been washed free and uncovered by the water which funneled down the path when it rained, she pulled herself to the crest of the ridge and found herself alone at the summit. The tops of the exposed gnarled roots showed the wear of the thousands of footsteps which had crossed them, the outer surface phloem of the vascular cambium polished smooth.

Many times she had climbed this mountain path with her father, centuries before as a child, and he had told her the names of the trees and the wild flowers, fungi that grew in the shades of the trees, which herbs and plants were medicinal in nature, and which contained natural emollients or oils which could be harvested and infused with the scent of flowers and leaves that grew on this small mountainside amidst the towering cedars. Ancient sentinels stood along the hiking footpath. In the forest dwelt songbirds which he could name and describe, the plumage and then their songs and where to look about the edges of the clearings where the birds and wildlife might occur, so that she could understand the habits of these edge species, and the nesting places in which they hid. The colors, the patterns, the staccato chatter or trilling melodies, the looping flights, or the upside down climbing on the barks of trees, the almost silent whoosh of owl's wings and the plaintive hooting sounds they made, the nest and mounds of the surface creatures making patterns on the loamy surface of the forest floor. It was from her father, and from his father before him, that her interest turned and was formed from the forest floor and the abundant life, all shaded by the canopy of trees. It turned into the formal science that she wrapped around her childhood memories and desires, like the embrace of her father as he stopped along the forest paths to teach her what he understood and loved. These were the things which they discovered together along forest footpaths like this. The memory of his arms embraced her.

Within his hands held the petals of a flower or the leaves and stem of a plant which she bent her head down to see as he spoke to his child about the external natural world that surrounded her. In this they experienced the wonder about them, in the forests and in the mountains, like an eternal external religion which they worshipped together in nature's outdoors, among the arborescence of a living Waldweg, a forest path, alive.

Now she returned to the present time and she was in the midst of runners ascending to a ridge. From here, the more-gentle side of the forest continued. As she crested the ridge, she began her own slow run down a footpath, here smoothed by pebbles and small rocks that littered the way down from the ridge above and behind her. She felt the freedom and lightness of foot as she ran down the steeply sloped surface, effortlessly carrying her weight as she passed runners working much harder with bowed heads and labored breaths climbing towards the crest that she had just left behind her.

Her unconscious concern for the stability of the Uinkaret caldera, the monogenetic vulcanism which underlay the environment to which the new society had migrated, somehow caused the restlessness of the dream sequence through which she found herself running. She continued to run effortlessly across the valley floor she now reached. Grassy fields lay on either side of her as she ascended the last hill, up towards the childhood home of her parents, long dead, with centuries of remembrance, and she found herself crossing the threshold of her parent's home. They rose from table as she entered the house, and they passed through the door into the living room. Her father's figure was now visible as he rose to greet her. Her mother followed behind him. Alfrieda stood in front of both of them, their arms reached out to meet their daughter, and her arms clasped around both of them. She fell to her knees and knelt in front of them as if she were a child, still clasping her arms about them as she began to cry, holding tight against their legs into which she buried her face. In the midst of her sorrow and her parent's embrace, the younger brother who had died as a child appeared within the embrace of the three, and now they were four.

Her effortless run had brought her to this home, and to this embrace of three now four, and she awoke with the start of tears trying to moisten her eyes. She imagined a rumble from deep within the tectonic plates of the Earth, as she shook herself to wakefulness. She wondered at the premonition, the meaning of the silent message from her parents and brother, all three centuries between them – gone. Her thoughts turned to the evening before and to Humboldt's Confederation speech, the acknowledged public proclamation of the formal commencement of the ARK project. Still attempting to shake off her deep sleep, she wondered whose father's arms would hold a child's attention in Haven.

xiv

The Great Salt Flats of Elysium were chosen for the site of the shuttle landings, an equatorial region extending nearly two thousand kilometers from west to east, a dried lake bed that had formed on the northern shore of the Great Southern Sea, formed as the land had risen over eons, as the weight of the great sea fell away from the equator, and collapsed the sea bed south. Great sea trenches formed to the west, carrying away the stabilizing weight of the water from the northern shore which had extended just above the equatorial line, now a dry, white, barren, forbidding desert area. The sea had fallen away. The briny water trapped beyond the receding shore had evaporated over millions of years, revealing a brilliant white surface, exceedingly flat, crusted over densely, impervious to the winds that traversed its surface which remained warmer than the land which surrounded it. There was nothing for hundreds of thousands of square kilometers but the desert whiteness of the desiccating salt, the remains of the former sea. The diatomic sea creatures which had photosynthesized on the sea's surface, now provided a calcified base to the salt crust which had formed over it. Thousands and millions and billions and trillions and quadtrillions of creatures over eons of time, converted the early atmospheric carbon dioxide and sea water to glucose, and pyruvate, releasing adenosine triphosphate by its unicellular respiration and oxygen, which eventually filled the atmosphere along with gaseous nitrogen and the now lessoned carbon dioxide. A uniform surface of thick salt was created which would support a fully loaded shuttle's weight of in excess of 100,000 kilograms.

Unable to transport heavy earth moving equipment across inhospitable space to the engineering colony in order to excavate a landing runway sufficient for the needs of shuttle landings, the engineering outpost had reconnoitered areas west and east, until it was determined that the Great Salt Flats surface was firm and dry enough to support a landing vehicle coming in at the speed and weight of the shuttle's planned configurations. An average three meters in thickness, the dense salt crust would provide a landing surface sufficiently long, wide, and stable enough to guarantee a safe incoming terminal for the human shuttle flights. In addition, south of this landing site was Lake Aeolis with its central mountain, the largest freshwater body on the surface of the planet yet discovered, south of the Great Salt Flats and surrounded by great tracts of arable land. From the salt flats to the lake was an area of gently rolling terrain, making the journey south to the lake settlement possible. It was an area with sufficient fresh water to provide for the growth of Haven to a population of 1.2 million people from the initial twenty thousand of the first generation to arrive from Earth, a planned six-fold doubling of the population over the next two Earth centuries of years, to a population numerous and diverse enough to survive natural disasters or disease, and a hoped for, an unspoken hope, that a potential cataclysmic end to humankind's source across interplanetary space would not cause Haven to fail.

The RMLF was completed for cargo flights, and robotic mission launches commenced from the facility which was built out to thirty launch pads, along with sixty return booster pads, which were simple reinforced concrete circular structures in which were embedded the electronic navigation controls which guided the descending 1st stage rockets returning back from the edge of space, after explosive bolt cutters freed them from the ascending 2nd stage boosters, moments before they ignited and catapulted the cargo spacecrafts into low Earth orbit. All this before the 2nd burn of the 2nd stage boosters whipsawed the crafts onto their elliptical orbital tracks which would allow them to intercept the orbit of Mars and then descend to its surface.

As the space port was built out to the final thirty launch pad facilities, every tenth pad was used each day on a rotating use schedule, until the frequency of launches reached three per day, to ensure that the ten thousand cargo flights could be completed, including the start-up phasing within a compressed twelve-year period.

The contents of cargo flights landing on Mars were initially brought to the engineering outpost. These supplies were needed by the outpost to support the construction of the ARK spaceport facilities which were to be located at the Great Salt Flats. Later cargo flights would land directly to the Salt Flats, and these materials would be transshipped to the Aeolis freshwater settlement site.

Heat shields of the incoming flights glowed incandescent as the cargo crafts slowed sufficiently before three supersonic drag chutes slowed and brought the crafts into vertical orientations. As the heat shields fell away, the 2nd stage engines still attached to the cargo craft began their third burns, as the rocket engines slowed the crafts and brought them to a 0.05 meter per second landing on the surface.

Once a cargo craft was on its landing pad, it would be stabilized, its descending fins locked onto the pad, the remaining navigational gases and flight crew compartment gases conserved. Propellant fuels were offloaded and conserved. Now the craft would be lowered to horizontal and removed from the landing pad. The 2nd stage engines, payload faring, and guidance module would all be transported to storage for later use and cannibalization, and the cargo would be removed for its intended use. Before the time that the frequency of cargo flights reached the three per day rate, manned human flights had already begun in order to staff-up the Martian engineering teams whose numbers alone were not able to manage the processing of the increasingly numerous cargo flights. The reception of all incoming flights, both cargo and human, now began to take place at the Salt Lake Space Reception Port. There were now enough new colonists that they would soon become self-sufficient in building Haven, allowing the resources of the engineering outpost to be devoted once again to the task of energy and mining production, and to act as an emergency support backup for the new, vulnerable, ARK of Haven.

xvi

Sensing the impending disaster, but not comprehending the speed of its denouement, Humboldt hurried back to his office and research compound. Calling in his immediate staff, he opened up and addressed the glowing holographic screens which monitored the entire activities of the Uinkaret infrastructure. With horror, but without a hint of its meaning escaping the expression from his face, the reverse Artemis curve began to take form on the screen illuminated in front of him. The doomsday curve, the beauty of its form, a mathematical theorem postulated, which had never escaped from the pages of a book, the calculation of a computer program, or the mind of a genius, now began to steady itself on the screen in his presence, like a scapegoat that refuses to run. Instructing his staff, all efforts began with which to steady the Uinkaret monitoring controls and keep the reporting parameters withing the upper and lower control limits. Contacting Alfrieda,

Konstantina, and Rotfach, he departed his office's control center and went immediately to the Social Entertainment Complex.

Konstantina and Alfrieda had planned far in advance of this day to support the ARK project with needed advice and guidance for the new Mars settlement. Their entire libraries and reference materials had already been sent on earlier missions, redundant archives were already on the surface, secured by the engineering team on planet in secure facilities for future reference. Rotfach, of course, was in place in temporary quarters which he maintained at the launch complexes. All four friends now gathered to relate what each of them had understood and observed, through their own functional organizations, and the progress with which they each had achieved their goals. None expected the news which Humboldt brought them, but all accepted that its possibility had arrived. Each tried to place their gallium arsenide chip-implanted wrist over the payment portal when their meeting concluded, a small shared fiscal act of generosity among the long beloved colleagues. Now was the time to conclude not only stalwart professional responsibilities, but to put one's personal affairs in order, and in the most bitter and ironic sense, to conclude with the final and irreversible chaos which was to follow, were the completion of the reverse Artemis curve to take place.

Neither Humboldt Noraxton, Alfrieda Praxis, Konstantina Oblation, nor even the engineering genius Rotfach Theoretrics would ever see the surface of Mars. But in an ironic twist of fate, the artist Shlater Curayan had managed a journey on one of the latest shuttle flights, applying for and being granted passage based on the multifaceted skills, practical knowledge, and expertise he had acquired using basic industrial tools and construction techniques as part of his formal arts education base. He possessed the ability to improvise creatively, an ability which was demonstrated while taking one of the battery of tests required for those being sent to the new planet. Shortly after, on another shuttle flight, Konstantina's daughter Zabana

Oblation would join Curayan there, also having demonstrated practical capabilities in the results of experiential and mental aptitude tests. The Confederation had acknowledged a tangential primacy of art in the historic development of man, from ancient human history to the present time, a need of expression and creativity, an appreciation of beauty in the human world, no matter how harsh. In time, Zabana would become charged with organizing a school of art, or at least a working trade atelier, which was also to support the settlement in any need and way possible using the practical skills of tools and construction taught as part of the curriculum of any School of Fine Arts.

It was not long after the final meeting of the four friends, that Humboldt experienced what would be his last act of love and recognition, and a final understanding of what would be lost. Long ago in a randomly selected, drug-induced dream sequence, he had been paired with a woman with whom he had been acquainted years earlier, but upon awakening from the dream sequence, his memory of the dream immediately faded. Hers held a brief recognition, but was not acted upon as she left the session with Humboldt. It is true that the unconscious mind within the state of dreams is uninhibited and can recognize genuine feelings. Many years earlier, these two individuals had worked together briefly in an academic laboratory class, and had nearly considered each as compatible for a first spousal partnership. But career demands upon a young person's head and heart can sometimes cause delay and an inability to act upon an emotional connection until that connection is lost. Now, despite these many years and centuries which in fact had taken place, they came together again, not in a drug-induced STA-like partnering at the Uinkaret Social Complex, but in Humboldt's private quarters. The woman had contacted Humboldt, knowing that this was now a last chance to re-kindle a relationship. The last days of Aadya and Humboldt would be spent together, and before the final human shuttle launch, a vial containing eight viable blastocysts would be safely stowed in a cryogenic container on board one of the last cargo launch vehicles. They would consummate Humboldt's all too short fifth spousal assignment, and leave beyond Earth's bounds the potential of a first child for both of them. They would never know, were a child of theirs to be born in a new world.

None of the four Confederation friends on Earth reached their full one thousand years. Each of them would experience the monogenetic vulcanism of the caldera event about which Humboldt had foretold, and which had provided the impetus for the immediacy of ARK, and rebirth on the fourth blue planet in Haven. Before the final cascading events, which would release and ignite not only the boiling caldera beneath the Uinkaret, other events never before considered in the settlement's disaster planning would lead to the uncontrolled release of thermonuclear materials which had powered their advanced civilization with limitless energy.

xvii

Superheated caldera gases, the cascading events of tectonic releases, and uncontrolled nuclear fusion from within a cloud of hydrogen gas escaped from magnetic near-absolute-zero fusion containment vessels, the vessels from which clean energy power had enabled the advancement of humankind, including the genetic research infrastructure which discovered, then allowed the development of lengthened lives. The combustion of the two engulfed the entire environs of the Uinkaret in a catastrophic ash of doom, and the entire planet spoke of the silence of lost technology.

In the Uinkaret's final moments, three human shuttle flights ascended from the Space Port HSLF. Three fiery contrails rose above the doomed city like a last judgement, pushed free from the deconstructing surface on its way to Haven, in tragic sight of the inverted pyramids of the great Interplanetary Confederation Hall from which Humboldt Noraxton had proclaimed its mission of hope and survival, disappearing above the columns of thundering whiteness upon which they rode into the eastern sky. Gyroscopic gallium arsenide guidance thrusters once again tipped the final speeding spacecrafts over to horizontal flight as they powered through MaxQ and attained low Earth orbit freefall, captured by the mass of the Earth's eternal gravity, unaffected by the extinction event which had begun to build below them on the surface. Then the final slingshot and farewell as the pressurized hypergolic fuels were forced into the three combustion chambers of the departing spacecraft, and spontaneously ignited for another burn in the three 2nd stage rocket engines. These final three crafts surged ahead, elongating the parabolic curve of their freefall orbit until they were released from the doomed third planet's gravitational pull. The last three Earthly flights of mothers and daughters, fathers and sons, sped onwards to Haven, across the vastness of interplanetary space, to be lost, unknown, into its own now singular time on planet Mars.

Far below and then above them as the craft began to rotate, following back from the unwinding arc of their trajectory, the caldera event had begun, ironically, in the place that man had sought his peace and freedom – Quaternary Uinkaret, Place of Peace, a coalescing meant to protect, enrich, and allow the development of lengthened lives and continue the history of humankind in its protective sanctuary. While it did all that, no one had predicted that there would be a price to pay which would take everything in return for that which they were enabled to achieve, and were able to send forth to live again. But it could not be known if it was to be a sending forth as random and unknown as the bringing together of the divided strands of DNA, if it was to be a sending forth like the unconscious mind of a developing child, who will have no memory of his parents if he does not survive the first few years of life, when his mind is not yet capable of their remembrance.

Over the next millennium, a layer of ash coalesced and settled upon every surface feature of the planet, while within the one hundred thousand square kilometers of the former Place of Peace, the Quaternary Uinkaret remained burned, blackened, and unrecognizable of previous human habitation, while winds carried aloft clouds of microscopic glassy particles of silicone dioxide to circle and temporarily cool the globe. In the center of this disaster the Uinkaret was buried under hundreds of meters of the caldera's volcanic materials – lost and erased from view of the surface world. A long shadow descended from the sky, decomposed to carbon blackness which itself was eventually covered over with the erosion sediment of another two hundred millenniums, with the arise of a new ice age in the northern latitudes, and the emergence of new life which had continued to survive elsewhere. Millennium upon millennium passed and no trace of the Uinkaret remained on the surface, buried too deeply to be discovered, mined, revealed, and recreated. Only strange and inconceivable tracings remained etched on the surface of the Earth in remote places on every continent, where stubborn tribes of the previous human culture who had refused the movement to the Uinkaret had survived and remained – cut-off, separated and isolated from one another, perceived but not understood, emerged from lost technologies which could image but not imagine their source or their meaning. These reaching out symbols of long-lost survivors, voluntarily exiled from or never coalesced to the Uinkaret, signaled and awaited a return and rescue from Haven which never took place. All these, whose meanings lay hidden, perished, lost, would remain to re-emerge once again, a long confusion of understanding to be rediscovered.

IV
Eden

i

For two hundred thousand years man stood on the fourth planet, planted the trees of life, and colonized every corner of the habitable new world's surface. But the first area to be colonized was south of the Great Salt Flats where flights had landed carrying the initial colonists who were charged, along with the crews of the engineering and mining complex, to consolidate the early cargo flights and colony work teams, and to build the first permanent settlement further south on the shores of Mars' great freshwater lake, Lake Aeolis. Lake Aeolis, the site of an ancient inactive volcano, within the middle of which rose the Mons, the central mountain of the geologic formation that spanned more than three hundred kilometers in diameter.

Certain industrial sites would be permanently built in the vicinity of the salt flats, due to the geologic stability of their immense deposits and the dense basalt foundation of the surrounding sublayers of the geography between the flats and Lake Aeolis. Here would remain the energy producing sites, the nuclear activity, and the infrastructure to produce and maintain the ore processing for fissionable products and for the capture and control of the fusion energy by-product – helium. An entire vertically integrated energy production industrial infrastructure would have to be built in order to provide one of the four essential needs of the settlement. Of the air, earth, fire, and water, this was the site of the fire which would fuel nearly everything else, the energy to survive, thrive, and to build a new Haven. This would be the source of fire for Haven, as was the sun for the entire solar system.

At the mountain which rose in the midst of Lake Aeolis, and in four other distributed Martian sites, the DNA codings of man, flora, and fauna were archived – the record of Earth life on land, in the air, and in the sea. Nine million life forms had been documented.

Twenty quadrillion base pairs of ACGT nitrogenous compounds for one hundred eighty billion total genes had been decoded, with an additional species documentation consisting of text and visual data. Fifty petabytes of data containing the ARK record of Earth's life were encapsulated in each of ten boules of inert pure silicon dioxide. Four were redundantly placed deep within the primary site of the mountain. The fifth one of these boules was accessible for use as a searchable data base at the original Mars settlement on the banks of Lake Aeolis. An additional four boules were archived in the quadrangles of Ismenius, Iapygia, Coprates, and Phaethontis, four regions geographically spread over the planet's topography.

There was one remaining depository not encapsulated and placed on the surface of Mars. It, too, contained the DNA mapping of every known Earth organism. This was a final lifeboat launch not destined for Mars. The tenth boule, within which was also the repository of decoded life on Earth, was launched into interplanetary space to fulfill the last covenant of the ARK project, and it was to be marooned for the ages as a final and last hope of eventual rescue. In addition, with great and vigorous debate, frozen receptacles containing human blastocysts, ovum, and sperm cells were loaded into a plutonium powered cryogenic container capable of maintaining a minimum temperature of minus one hundred ninety-six degrees Celsius, the temperature of liquid nitrogen, for a minimum period of seven years until the payload contents of the satellite craft reached an orbit around the sun at a distance of 20AU, three billion kilometers, to endlessly fall in orbit somewhere between the seventh and eighth planets. A cryogenic container powered by the electrical generation of radioisotopic heat enabled its frozen journey to the distant orbit in order to achieve a permanent interplanetary ambient temperature of minus two hundred degrees Celsius, in a one-hundred-five-year solar orbit. Were all else to fail on Mars, having already failed on Earth, perhaps human life could be retrieved out of the orbit around the distant sun by some future unknown descendant or interstellar race. Geologic guidance maps to this eternal orbit were carved into the surface of the Earth, the surface of Mars, in the interior of the great mount Aeolis Mons, and on the surface of each pure silicon dioxide boule, this tenth one of which accompanied, as final guardian, the capsules of actual frozen life. The record of Earth's DNA, and the nascent ability of human life to be born again, was placed into this spacecraft and prepared for its everlasting journey around the sun.

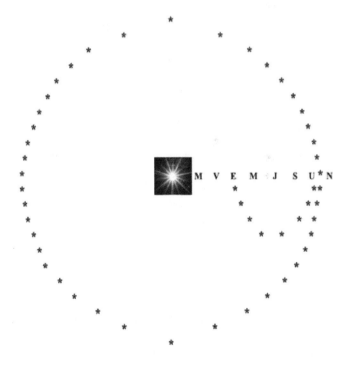

ii

The "Peace Drones" of Mars were designed and deployed to look outward to protect against incoming danger from asteroids, comets, or meteors calculated to be large enough to wreak havoc on the surface of the planet. They were intended to be constant sentinels scanning the heavens for objects that might breach the atmospheric protection of the planet and hurtle themselves toward the surface. Were any object calculated to be too massive to be consumed in an incandescent sublimation as it hurtled through the protective layer of nitrogen and oxygen, the weapons of the Peace Drones were intended to be deployed away from the surface of our planet to destroy any incoming extinction threat before it ever breached the Mars atmosphere.

Life cannot be denied, and with the life of humanity came the freedom to force its fate. The lifeline from the mother planet was cut with the collapse and destruction of the Uinkaret. It would require another two hundred millenniums for ARK to rise again to its previous level of Earthly development. Discoveries were lost, learning interrupted, famine and disease struck the vulnerable population, yet humankind would survive. The full measure of ten thousand flights to Mars would not be completed. Haven would not be fully funded. And through it all, the believing spirits of all those colonists who had made the journey, would come to inhabit Haven. They would do so with the certainty in their knowledge that all who made this collective journey would find their new Haven on Mars, as had the initial travelers and the members of the permanent engineering and mining colony that had preceded them on Earth's first interplanetary adventure.

iii

The great salt flats north of Lake Aeolis stretched farther than one could see in any direction, composed of the evaporated deposits of potassium, magnesium, and sodium chloride, the result of millions of years of photosynthetic processes and mineral leaching. Magnesium was contained in the center of each molecule of the dark green ester chlorophyll, potassium was released into the former sea by the decomposition of dead vegetation, and sodium and chlorine ions were leached from geologic minerals in Mars' crust. Further beyond, hundreds of kilometers in the distance, ranges of the Elysium mountains could be seen to the north. Turning to the southeast, only the exception of the single mount of Aeolis Mons rose in the distant southeast, a leveling flatness which rolled up and back out to meet your gaze. The brilliant whiteness of the flats met the cerulean sky at the horizon, in a boundary defined with the sharpness of the edge of a blade. Beyond this blinding whiteness of nothingness, the sum total of all colors, the perception of color itself washed away over the desiccated landscape, and beyond the distant view lay a great fertile plain which surrounded the crater of the Mons. Invisible beyond the curve of the planet, lapped the shore of the Great Southern Sea, in the nearness of which could sometimes be felt and sometimes be detected the scent of the sea.

Hundreds of thousands of years earlier, the last great volcanic eruption on Mars had occurred which formed the crater lake, Lake Aeolis, first captured as a salt water basin. Over eons of time, sodium and chloride ions flowed into the formation of the Great Southern Sea, leached out of surface rocks by carbolic acid created when rain dissolved the atmospheric carbon dioxide. After the sea regressed and retreated from the rim of the Mons crater, plankton-like cellular creatures which had populated the upper layers of the waters, died out as salination increased, then the remnants of the sea itself dried completely with an outflow which occurred as one of many earthquakes created a breach in the rim of the crater. Dry for centuries, the Mons crater eventually refilled, this time with the fresh water precipitated on the mountains to the east, and gradually became the largest freshwater system on the planet, with a path connected like a string of pearls to the smaller lakes which were linked by the canals and streams which followed the islands from the great western trench, the Valles Marineris east, all the way to the Mons and beyond.

iv

Inbound flights from Earth had already ceased, the two shuttle landings every third day, and the two daily cargo flights were replaced with silence. Humboldt's 50-year plan had quickly become a 40-year plan, with a ten-year allowance for the inevitable difficulties that would be encountered. And as the Uinkaret had become less stable, that 40-year plan was compressed to an impossible 10-year plan. The Interplanetary Confederation had given Rotfach's project teams a new seemingly impossible schedule, Rotfach was not asked what could be achieved, it was commanded to the technologist what must be done. Despite all efforts, the completion of this goal would not be fully carried out. There would not be possible sufficient flights to the new colony for the completion of even a minimal infrastructure. Only a temporary survival of the new inhabitants could be guaranteed. Workshops had only been constructed for the most minimal of essential needs of Haven. Agricultural activities had commenced, and the emergency stores of foodstuffs and medical supplies were safely stockpiled in a doomsday vault – insurance against a catastrophe during the early years of Haven. The initial two long-life generational needs had been safely achieved only because a lessor population of colonists had been able to immigrate from Earth before all flights ceased when the Uinkaret was lost. Beyond the first two generations much would have to be achieved without assistance from the mother planet. There was a great risk of loss of technological capability and the culture of human achievement. There was a risk of a descent into a dark age which could span millenniums in a world made hostile by the demands of the new, unknowable, unnatural nature of Mars.

The preliminary settlement structures on the dry lake bed were eventually moved and reassembled near the great Lake. Workshops transitioned, and a new Uinkaret gradually rose to accommodate the new colonists. The believers in the new world began to create the new Haven on Mars. They had believed in the promise of human migration, the belief in a willing spirit, and in the instincts of survival on the other side of interplanetary space in a new world. One thousand three hundred eighty-two human shuttle flights had been launched, and of these voyages, nineteen of the launches required the interplanetary abandonment of one ship to the other, so that twenty colonists, not ten, exited each of the nineteen rescue ships that landed on the Great Salt Flat. Unfortunately, half of the colonists on each of these nineteen rescue ships were unable to bring their personal cargo with them from the abandoned ships. Thirty-one ships had been lost, a 2.2% failure rate, with the deaths of three hundred ten passengers. Thirteen thousand five hundred ten souls made the successful journey from Earth to Haven. Over six thousand cargo flights of the eight thousand planned, achieved the journey to Mars. The earliest and most critical cargo had been ferried to the planet, but the failure to achieve all eight thousand planned flights meant austerity, and a critical new survival modus operandi. And now, circling the sun between the seventh and eighth planet, was the last lifeboat craft carrying the sum of Earth's DNA, and the potential cryogenic life of hundreds of thousands more, were the ingenuity of man or some interplanetary or interstellar traveler capable of harnessing that orbiting spacecraft in the possibility of a far distant future.

The dry lakebed proved to be the best location at which to store the supplies and space vehicles themselves that landed there. These were prepared for storage until the material, equipment, and supplies brought by other cargo ships could be consolidated and reassembled into buildings and machinery equipment. The shuttle vehicles and cargo ships became the raw materials for use of the Haven colonists. The fuselages of the shuttle vehicles were removed from the craft and transported to the settlement area lakeside at the Mons, and became the barracks and apartments for the colony. They were

connected and stacked to form living quarters for the first and
second generations as the new society developed.

For the first time in human history, agriculture and
industrialization would be developed at the same time. Never
before had both been implemented as side-by-side
technologies. Unlike man's evolution and development on
Earth, there would be no need of a linear progression from one
to the other. The efficient means of production and storage of
agricultural products enabled enough workers for both the
fields and factories. Like the building of a factory first before
the machines are installed, the first order of agriculture was to
secure the doomsday seed vault in the southern, near polar
region of Phaethontis, the site of which would also contain one
of the DNA boules, the compendium of Earth life. Within the
seed vault was contained the most important plant species as
determined by the agricultural committee which had reported
to the Interplanetary Confederation over which Humboldt had
presided. These live embryonic receptacles of the flora species
brought from Earth were safeguarded to preserve and protect
against a potential catastrophic biological plague or other
nonbiological disaster, which might destroy essential plant
stocks and doom the colony to starvation and extinction.

One great mystery of Mars was that although there were
species of flora found throughout the planet, there was a total
absence of fauna – with the exception of the microscopic
creatures of the sea, and the nitrogen fixating bacteria in the soil
– the total absence of which could not be explained. It was in
great contrast to how life and the source of great consciousness
had evolved on Earth, and the ages of evolution required to
develop it. It posed questions more eternal than those
considered before this puzzle was discovered – enabled by the
ebb and flow of interplanetary travel now within man's reach,
and interstellar travel which could now be imagined. The first
Mars universal ancestor had produced a lineage through its
billions of years which excluded conscious-capable fauna.
What it did produce was a diversity of plant species which were
all by necessity asexual in the absence of insects and flower-

feeding birds. It evolved oxygen producing photosynthetic diatomic plankton of the sea, and nitrogen fixating bacteria which produced ammonia-nitrogen trihydride – the building block of RNA and DNA – and amino acids for proteins produced by plant biosynthesis. Bacteria containing enzymes produced catalysts of iron, molybdenum, and vanadium in order to draw the nitrogen out of the air, hydrogen from water molecules, and in exchange release oxygen to the atmosphere. Diatomic phytoplankton, living within silicate cell walls, produced photosynthetic carbohydrates which fueled their organisms while producing atmospheric oxygen. Photosynthesis was the source of energy for all living flora on the planet Mars, the same source of energy for all the flora and fauna on Earth. The chemical process essential to all forms of life – photosynthesis – had enabled a symbiotic cycle of nitrogen fixing bacteria, oceanic diatoms, and the plant life that evolved to cover the planet.

Reconnaissance parties were formed after the settler shuttles arrived, and were outfitted with materials brought by the initial cargo crafts. They explored the areas south of the salt beds and made their way to Lake Aeolis. This area, the equatorial region where the climate was temperate, was most similar to the temperatures of the regions north and south of the equator on Earth, the regions of the tropical latitudes defined by the farthest north or south tilt of the planet on its annual orbit around the sun. Compensating for the additional eighty million kilometers distance from the sun, the higher concentration of carbon dioxide and a corresponding decrease in nitrogen in the atmosphere of Mars compared to Earth, allowed the planet to capture and retain the heat of the more distant sun. The increased density of carbon dioxide in the atmosphere, 1.8% versus the Earth's 0.4%, accounted for the lushness of the vegetation, the increased temperature of the waters of the Great Southern Sea, and perhaps in an unknown process, the absence of animal life. The lush foliage enabled by the higher concentration of carbon dioxide over the eons, had produced the temperate climate on this, the more distant blue/green orb of the fourth planet.

What had favored flora over fauna, now enabled humankind to walk on an acceptably hospitable surface. For hundreds of kilometers between the great salt flat and the Aeolis Lake, were lush fields of a grain like vegetation, which bent with gentle equatorial winds that moved across its undulating surfaces. With only 38% of the gravity on Earth, the grain bearing stalks of the most common plants covered fields of immense size with an odd appearance compared to the grain crops of Earth. Apparently monoecious, the double rows of tiny flowers on each of the three-sided stalks yielded three double rows of large, strangely shaped grains, forming heads so heavy they could not have been supported if exposed to the gravity on Earth. These grains resembled the rows of kernels on an ear of corn, where the female carpels are fertilized and developed. Along the stalks on three sides below the flower bearing heads were leaves like the fins of a fish which extended the length of the slender three-meter stalks. Where the leaves reached the stamen flowers, they extended along both their sides, not higher than the petals of the flowers, open to the air. But where the fins of leaves met the carpels, they enclosed themselves smoothly encasing the developing grains within, once the fertilization had taken place, and the kernels of the grain began to form inside the leaves which folded over them.

The effect with even a gentle wind was an almost silent rattling as the heads of the stalks moved against each other, a gentle murmur, a susurrus of sound which extended audibly, delicately, as far as the eye could see and the ear could hear, a constant chattering sound as if insects on each stalk created their sounds with the rhythm of respiration.

Through these enormous grain fields, the settlers proceeded to their fresh water settlement, where they would build their new, permanent city. Earth moving equipment from the Mars mining outpost was brought over to the Salt Flats to make the roadway from the flats to Aeolis Lake. With just over one third of the weight of the materials to be moved, compared to what the weight of the same materials would have been on Earth's surface, the load bearing requirement of the highway, and the energy required to move the materials made the task still difficult, but more manageable than it otherwise would have been. The relative strength of man and machine was roughly tripled versus that on Earth, due to the lessor gravity of Mars.

Much of the spacecraft materials were chosen to be put into protective storage on the salt flats in the open dry air for future use. A linear equation was worked out to describe the order of use of the materials brought to Mars, the use of which materials needed to provide for all needs of the first two generations of natural births. Redundancy, and secondary redundancy of resource planning had been completed. During the initial colonialization activity, which had been expected to take the first two generations of time to complete, materials and spacecraft seemed to pile up in quantities not capable of being used or consumed. The Fifty-Year Plan had been communicated by Humboldt Noraxton at the Confederation Headquarters at the Uinkaret, a plan conservatively imminent (with the hope of a hundred years), but in subsequent years, the number of failures to the plan cascaded to near chaos. Meanwhile, in the rumblings from across the interplanetary chasm, the Earth's volcanic caldera activity foretold first the stressful societal dissolution, then the fast follow of a remorseless, ruthless, relentless destruction of the Uinkaret, a destruction as iron-hearted as the metallic core of Earth from which the fires of the caldera burst forth. The remaining scheduled flights of cargo and colonists, the final transfer of man and the goods and tools by which to survive on Mars, ceased.

With the exception of the most primitive, few, and far-flung wilderness survivors who had refused for generations to access the Earth's Uinkaret and submit to its order, who had no chance nor desire of communication on Earth or to the heavens, the peoples of the ARK at Haven were now utterly alone, marooned in isolation within the entirety of the solar system's heliosphere.

V

Lieutenant Colonel Rudi Oestrum was in the third tour of duty on the surface of Mars, the commander of the first permanent Martian engineering mining outpost. The colonization manifest was a series of voluminous specification documents which tracked the order of movement for each cargo and human spacecraft launched from Earth, the contents of either cargo or colonists, the receipt and usage or storage and registration of each item brought to the fourth planet, and the intended task of each passenger received there.

It was Commander Oestrum's mission to organize the work parties and to complete the mission steps according to the colonization manifest, to the best of the ability of the military work teams under command. In light of the always possible or frequent need to reinterpret the mission objectives based on changing conditions on the ground, the completion of the mission required the ability to successfully improvise tasks to achieve the strategic goals in light of unforeseen circumstances. Where the details needed to be changed, the purpose was to achieve as similar a result as was the goal of the original plan.

The broad sequence of planned events was crucial to the success of Haven. The order of receipt of the incoming spacecraft, whether human or cargo needed to be met with the conditions on Mars that were suitable for their receptions. All of the spacecraft carried either an essential, irreplaceable component, one for which there was no substitute or alternative, or a passenger whose specific skills would be difficult to replace. These essential components and skills had to be considered so that a subsequent flight within a required timeframe would be able to provide the complementary skill or component. Examples might be special handling equipment required for servicing nuclear batteries, skills related to medical procedures or specific technological expertise in geological, biological, or digital technologies. It might require knowledge of quantum mechanics in support of artificial intelligence, or complex architectural procedures involving linear equations. These were skills and experience that could not be practiced and acquired merely by consulting the voluminous and complete specification documentation supplied to the new society.

The orders presented to the Lieutenant Colonel were unequivocal, a manifest of survival, the ability to design, manufacture, and use the infrastructure required for modern humankind, in a new many billions-year-old world where nothing human had ever existed before. Like an earlier Earth, before humans had tread the surface, this was a developed natural world, after eons of calamitous and violent eras of creation, but a world still silent without the rise of conscious fauna. Yet it was a world receipt for inhabitation, a pristine garden with an abundance of natural beauty.

There would be a heroic struggle to achieve essential skills and knowledge. Large, complex infrastructure equipment which could not have been sent preassembled from Earth, had to be redesigned, built, and installed on Mars. The consequences of not having received these things would not be experienced in the early years of the settlement colony. The needs of the new settlers were fully provided for by the initial food and supplies which had arrived on cargo craft. The possibility of that terrible realization would come later, and be evident in the midst of a sleepless Martian night, when even with the unaided naked eye, any member of the new society could look towards the tiny blue-green disk rising in the east and perceive a change in the first magnitude of its appearance from across the vast interplanetary space between them.

Commander Oestrum addressed the members of the military staff assembled in one of the shuttle fuselages repurposed for the use of the Strategic Command Council. The Commander had now been on the surface of the planet for thirteen years, ten years after the first new settlement flights had begun. The original outpost/mining mission orders were to have lasted five Earth years before a scheduled return to Earth. But after five years of reduced gravitational effect, one year in flight, and four

Earth years on the surface of Mars, it would have required an equal number of years on Earth before a return to Mars would have been possible. No one had yet achieved a new enlistment on Mars after returning to Earth. The reduced gravity effects on the human body were found to be too long lasting after so many years of reduced gravity on the surface of the smaller planet, combined with the years of confined travel. It was an impossible physical sacrifice. At the end of the first five years to Mars, with the learned and adaptive ability to cope with the lower gravitational effects, the Commander chose to stay on mission, effectively making the decision to live out the rest of a dedicated military life on the planet, in service to the goal of the first new second society in human history. A worthy cause, and one in which the interest was so stimulated, it seemed no sacrifice. Instead, it was perceived to be a worthy adventure in which to invest a willing and eager military life.

It was not yet known how the gravitational effects would or would not influence the longer life gene which resided in each of the outpost beings. The Commander was still relatively young, only at the beginning of a third century of life, born in 9735. At only two hundred and twenty-seven years old, there were no children, nor had the Commander chosen any spousal partners, having been satisfied with the therapies provided by society to those with or without partners. It allowed more concentration on a career and the missions in which to participate. Perhaps selfishly, there had been no time to invest in a more permanent relationship or to think about being the parent of a child. Perhaps it was an effort that there was just no desire to give, because in the absence of war and combat which was no longer the scourge of human society, there was in fact more time for such a relationship. A relationship with a spousal partner could last longer than the length of any individual military assignments. And there were many who had no confidence that a relationship would remain stable through the course of multiple deployments. Perhaps in selfishness, the Commander thought, there was simply no reason, no need to share the energy required to enlist in new assignments, with the bridging of a relationship between new assignments and the consistent energy with which it was required to invest in such a relationship. Besides, it was always possible to fraternize with military colleagues of similar rank with limited emotional investment, and there were no longer any of the ancient prohibitions which had frowned upon such behavior. Under the duress of psychologically difficult and dangerous missions, emotional involvement with a significant other was not truly possible. Within-rank limited emotional relationships were found to be more productive to intellectual stability, than that which was achieved only by countenance of abstinence and the use of social services. Perhaps the practice of taking temporary front spouses in certain ancient military cultures had satisfied a necessary emotional expedient after all. In any event, for those individuals such as Commander Oestrum who chose no personal attachments with spousal partners, the sexual therapy allowances and the occasional military fraternization provided sufficient physical and emotional satisfaction.

"Gentlemen," she began, using the address to colleagues both female and male which no longer had the meaning to identify the sex of the recipient, the divisiveness of gender references with which ancient society struggled was now long forgotten.

"We have begun the second decade of the Confederation's covenant dedicated to the establishment of the ARK at Haven."

After thirteen years on the new planet, the cartilage in her spine and between each joint of her body had expanded, and her stature was no longer bound in the same way by the two and one-half times greater gravity on Earth's surface. Her stature had always been domineering, but now had become even more so. Her 1.88m height and 61kg on Earth had increased to 1.99m on the surface of Mars, maintaining her athletic Earth weight of 61kg. Her blue-grey eyes now more closely matched the color of her gradually changing blonde hair, short in the military style, not required but practical. She bore the phenotype complexion and coloring of an ancient northern genotype.

Broad shouldered for a woman – even for a woman of her height and athletic ability – her upper body strength accentuated and was set upon a short waisted torso, and her long legs still reminded one of the athleticisms with which she had possessed on the playing field. Now she demonstrated a strength and ease of movement, leading difficult military maneuvers for the women and men under her command in the field. She had a casual way of speaking but with a clipped military precision which left no doubt she was accustomed to command. She wore the convenience of military issued clothing, and despite her physical size, her overall appearance was one of a disciplined frugality, but not one of asceticism or deprivation. She was clearly provided for within the simplicity of her chosen lifestyle.

"We have now offloaded all of the materials which will allow us over the next thirty-plus years, the materials and equipment with which to begin to rebuild a new and complete society here, with the technological equivalence to our Earth's Quaternary Uinkaret."

"Think for another moment what this means. Think of the things with which you required for the use at your homes in your everyday lives in the Uinkaret. Every object you touched, every surface upon which you walked, each item or service which you requested by speech or movement which responded to your demands, the food stuffs which we processed, preserved, and ate. All of this will require the building of a new vertical infrastructure which must be built here in Haven upon which our future generations will depend."

"The most precious of all our possessions which were first to be sent here, and which were immediately prepared for archival protection – our encapsulated DNA records of Earth life forms, and the seed vaults – have all been secured. All are monitored by our central command, secured and safe, a compendium of the biological history of our past human existence on Earth and the living embryonic seeds of those mapped DNA plant species which we've chosen to bring with us."

"Everything upon which our existence has depended came from the soil, air, water and fire of our mother Earth. Now we will make use of these same resources here from the Martian soil, air, water, and fire – from the mined ore to steel, from crushed rock to glass, from the introduction of plants to the harvest, from a knowledge of chemistry and physics to energy and the synthesis of materials, from the art of mathematics, science, and architecture, to the building of infrastructure and new cities."

And in a nod perhaps to what most separated the rise of humankind from the Earth's animal kingdom.

"And from the desire to find and explore the meaning of existence in the humanities, the compulsion to express the appreciation of beauty in the continuation of the fine arts."

vi

As the frequency of seismic activity continued its gradual increase at the Uinkaret, Alfrieda Praxis noted that the P-S BodyWave charts on this phenomenon more frequently reached towards the upper control limits, perhaps presaging the beginning of an earthquake swarm. Most of these surface wave tremors remained undetected by the general public, the activity of which passed without an acknowledgement of physical manifestation from the two great underground caldera reservoirs. And throughout each minute of each day, trapped beneath the tectonic weight of the Earth's crust, the volcanic magma chambers underneath the Uinkaret continued their slow expansion, their filling up for the letting out which would come again as it had come before in the vast geologic history of the second blue orb, Earth, the third planet of the solar system.

Alfrieda was reminded of the primitive camping she enjoyed in the rugged outdoors surrounding the Uinkaret. The communing with nature away from the city and the city's offerings, whether it be shelter, or sustenance, or entertainment. Here in nature, an enjoyment of simple human activities – days filled with only the ease of rising beneath the spreading sky, a simple breakfast of cooked grain and coffee, walking, hiking, climbing through a natural wilderness, resting and eating the natural complex carbohydrates of dried fruits and nuts. And at the end of a day spent only in the surroundings of nature, dependent on the solar cycle, not the clock, to make camp and refresh one's self with another simple meal and a boiled drink, and to sleep again under the canopy of stars, needing only the things brought with her in the pack on her back.

Then in a dream come gently with the exertion of the day, her unconscious mind imagined a forty-year wilderness outing with a magic pack containing provisions that multiplied to satisfy her needs spanning four decades. At the end of her long trek her pack was empty, the contents of which was no longer replenished. She imagined that the Uinkaret from which she had come at the beginning of her trek was no longer there. Nothing but an empty wilderness remained, awaiting her return. Now after these forty years, all upon which she had formerly depended needed to be rediscovered and reproduced. That had been the work of the centuries and millenniums of her forebears, those who had made the discoveries which spread in multiple linear sequences as one discovery led to another, like the way the names written down spread out on the limbs of a family tree. There was often no understanding by what use there might be in a newly discovered knowledge. Now the end uses were understood for all the myriad things seen and unseen that supported modern life, but to have to recreate that infrastructure of knowledge, to be able to reacquire the physical capability in which to produce the things of modern technological life – this was a possibility of overwhelming complexity. To know what the end use is, but to have to imagine how to rebuild what was gained over millions and billions of man-years of effort, of both random natural selection followed by directional intellectual effort! It was entirely possible – we had the specification documents of the colonization manifest – to recreate a new world on Mars, were there still the Uinkaret together with its assistance from which to build another. But to imagine the Uinkaret having been lost before your return from a forty-year exile, and have to recreate it all without assistance in an abandoned wasteland…

Alfrieda awoke ungently, unrefreshed from her slumber beneath the stars visible above her transparent canopy.

The fragrance of sagebrush permeated the fabric of her tent, and the inner surface began to glow as the sun, still below the horizon, gradually illuminated the sky. In the dry atmosphere of the Uinkaret, days were warm, and nights were cool – not as extreme as the desert to the west, but this was still high desert country, and the chill in the tent was already beginning to be displaced by the warming air outside.

Alfrieda unzipped the door of her tent. The moon was setting in the western sky, the sun was still beneath the opposite horizon, and Venus was fading from view as the lightening sky overwhelmed its magnitude. She stepped outside her fabric structure. Fresh air breathed upon her face. She could see the bed her tent had formed in the sagebrush. She stood in the freshness that surrounded her, and moved to an open space on the ground where she lit her stove.

She was thankful that the taste of the coffee which she prepared was richer and more satisfying than it had been the previous morning in her flat, and before she finished drinking from the cup of double walled titanium which held her steaming drink, she felt within her pack to reassure herself that there was still plenty of coffee to last for the rest of her trek along with the fuel container with which to heat the water.

Earth, wind, fire, and water.

vii

The first order of business had long been understood. Oestrum understood. The climate of Mars was conducive for humankind's survival. The atmosphere's content of oxygen at sea level was sufficient for life, despite the one third Earth's gravity which still bound it to the surface of the planet. Nitrogen percentage lower, carbon dioxide higher, an enabling greenhouse effect that warmed the planet even though its distance was fifty percent farther than the sun's distance to Earth. Forty-some percent of the direct radiation that the Earth received, equalized by the lens of carbon dioxide which also provided a moderating effect of daylight versus nighttime temperatures and the efficacy of longwave electromagnetic radiation reflected off the ionosphere. The presence of benign photosynthetic and nitrogen fixating bacteria and diatomic life forms, and the waves of grain yielding flora enriched the fertile soils of the equatorial regions. The absence of mammals, birds, fishes, reptiles, amphibians, and insect life forms was puzzling. Perhaps an undetected radiation condition which prevented a progression of conscious life forms in an earlier age of the planet. Or perhaps an undetected extinction event which had occurred at some point in the three billion years of the sister planet's journey around the sun, which destroyed the delicate chemistry of the more complex DNA of higher life forms?

Even at the cellular level, life proceeds with the energy produced in the mitochondria of its cells. Fire must be first. The energy of life. A synthesizing lightning. It is one thing to create a fire from the friction of a combustible substance. Iron can be produced by a carbon fueled fire stoked in the hearth. But to harness the energy of split or fused atoms, the energy source required for a technological society – the daunting task of the creation of fire would be first.

Even the most basic metal making technology requires expert knowledge. Tungsten, a nonferrous element with the highest melting point of any known metal, essential in a nuclear society, requires the hottest flame to be able to work its difficult ductile properties, and to swage it into rods and then to be thinly or thickly drawn for electrical or electronic applications through diamond dies. Its density can be suitable for high velocity ballistic applications, or combined with other metals like steel for the production of alloys for use in high temperature applications. It is an essential metal for rocket engines, reentry surfaces, or the cores and dies for high temperature production of inert glass materials made of the purest silicone dioxide used in semiconductor production, tooling required for the use of any society of advanced technology, reactor and containment vessels. Tungsten carbide materials are used in the production of precision metal working tools for the cutting and processing of other metal products. And its coefficient of expansion is among the lowest of any substance at the highest working temperatures required for precision casting, molding, and drawing processes. Tungsten is able to withstand the heat and violence generated by the friction of reentry vehicles. All this is possible if you have the knowledge and mechanics with which to mine the tungsten ores, concentrate them, and precipitate various states of the element in batch processes until you have finally precipitated the element into an oxide form which can then be reduced to the pure metal and water, after lehring in a sealed furnace containing a pure hydrogen atmosphere.

In the two generations planned time frame of the Mars settlement, this was just one of the requirements which had been taken into account by the planning teams reporting to Rotfach Theoretrics. A small detailed example within the multiple linear progressions of development needed to meet the requirements of specific industries or technologies. There was a multiplex of concurrent developments of associated complimentary technologies so that at the end of the assisted development phase, the minimum infrastructure would be in place, allowing further independent development from the pioneers on Mars.

In the private conversations of the friends – Humboldt, Alfrieda, Konstantina, and most of all Rotfach – there had always been the fear of what the omission of even one key technological capability would mean to the new society on the planet. They had always understood that the only certain outcome, the only certain result of human planning and intentions for the new world on Mars would be that the outcome or result would not be what was planned or intended. The concern expressed by these friends on Earth was not that something would go wrong. It was that there was no knowing what it was that would go wrong, be omitted entirely, forgotten, or what might be destroyed during its implementation. There was one thing that they had all agreed upon that was the most important ingredient that must be recognized in human planning – that planning activities are never complete or all-knowing. But they believed that the human spirit would attempt at all costs to prevail in spite of all difficulty, not just in the hopes of mere survival, but in the sure knowledge that at some unknown time in an unknowable future, the mothers and daughters, fathers and sons with their collective human spirit, would ascend on planet Mars to live again at the highest levels of the Uinkaret from which they had come.

viii

The settlement progressed, and the area surrounding the extinct volcanic mountain at Lake Aeolis was also settled, and within its great mass the boules of the DNA repository – now archived – lay deep within the structure carved into the igneous rock. One remained at the settlement, accessible for research, while four were placed in the regional quadrangles. On the polished stone surfaces of the archive chambers, the art of Zabana Oblation and Shlater Curayan would record the history of Earth and the journey to Mars, the depiction of the solar system and planets. The frozen orbit of the lifeboat craft containing cryogenically preserved life, at a distance of twenty Astronomical Units from the sun would also be represented on the walls of the archive, a small Earth satellite circling the sun for the eternity of its existence or until its recovery, sailing between the orbits of Uranus and Neptune. Their depictions represented the human spirit paused with potential for a new life. Were the essence of this lifeboat ever called back into a conscious existence, the legacy of the anonymous mothers and fathers would be captured from its eternal orbit. The final redundant hope of a temporarily displaced race to ascend again, from the surface of the second blue orb which had given it life.

Trees and fruits were planted, euryhaline fishes raised from the frozen roe of one of the last shipments from Earth, hatched, and were released into the freshwater Lake Aeolis to make their way south to the salt water sea, returning as anadromous spawning caviar-filled adults. Grains were harvested, and the new dominion of a new planet began. Years after their project began deep within the Mons, Shlater and Zabana and the assistants, students, and apprentices of their atelier completed their work. The Genetic Containment Doors behind which were contained the four boule DNA archives and Record of Life on Earth were sealed, sealed again, and sealed through the third set of blast hardened GCD's which opened onto the mountain side.

Of the twenty thousand colonists planned for the settlement on Lake Aeolis, only two were professional artists of the ten thousand that were able to travel there. But many of the skilled engineers and other professionals chosen for the new world were also amateur artists, musicians, and other patrons of the arts. Zabana and Shlater would establish the Lake Waters Atelier and its classes would include instruction in all art forms. Large instruments had not been able to be brought to the planet, but small stringed, woodwind, and brass instruments had been brought aboard the shuttle flights. Electronic synthesizers were fashioned to replace the larger instruments not permitted to be brought on board the shuttles. The Atelier proved to be one of the most important gathering places for the new colonists. Amateur performances of some quality were eventually capable of being presented to an appreciative public. This was another aspect of an ascending human spirit which now took place across the interplanetary divide between the second and third blue planets, in an almost holy expression of what it was to be human.

Interestingly enough, it was Rotfach who had been a fervent advocate in favor of the arts content of the new society, even though the harder and more practical primary skills were of the utmost importance to the survival on the new planet. The infrastructure build-out was paramount for the continuation of the survival of the colonists. But to his friends, Rotfach also remembered the description of the meaning of music that had been included in the program of a long-ago concert at the Uinkaret entertainment complex.

He was just a young boy, and he had never before heard such music from the open-air proscenium that had been built into the hill outside of the Social Entertainment Complex. He had never forgotten that music, and when he was older, and had studied music as an amateur musician, the complexity and humanity of the expression he had heard as a boy always stayed with him. Whenever he himself performed with his student groups, or when he practiced alone, it was the humanity of music which moved him. From a composer's life, long ago before the advent of genetic technology which removed diseases that shortened the lives and experience of man, a singular genius of towering intellect spoke through the emotion and lyrical order of his music. The eternal goodness of humankind's nature was expressed in spite of the humility forced upon the composer by the ailments with which he suffered. Ailments which no longer existed to create human suffering, already unknown for centuries by the time Rotfach first heard the ancient music, along with the libretto's power of the words which accompanied a final performing chorus. Long before wars had ended and human physical suffering had been abated, the ancient composer who suffered deafness, had risen above the condition of man to celebrate the joy of life. His words and music embraced the millions, the sons and daughters of joy in the source of life, long before the mystery of genetic life science was discovered. It was as if a prescient prayer for the certainty of what was yet unknown, and which would remain undiscoverable for centuries, for millenniums, to come.

Rotfach Theoretrics had never forgotten the music which he had heard as a schoolboy. He was pleased that the life of the arts would continue, even as limited by the amateur musicians among the population of scientists and engineers of the ARK.

They had of course been chosen for their technological capabilities required for the building of Haven, and not for their musical talents. Few of the colleagues with whom Rotfach worked knew of him as an amateur musician. The circle of friends with whom he played with was not large. There was a divide between those who played electronic instruments, and those who played instruments resonated by breath, vibration, or percussion. What could not have been produced thousands of years ago, before the beginnings of the electronic revolution, would have been considered marvels of unimaginable value, he mused, to the musician of ancient times, the rarest possession of an inestimable worth. The irony of it, he thought, was that now it was a tangible instrument which could be held and felt within your hand, resonated by breath, vibration, or percussion, even if produced by machine, that held the most intrinsic value. A most brilliant engineer, a genius of mathematical design and application to technology, what still moved Rotfach most deeply was the art of music. It held an emotional attachment to him. The complexity of design of the infrastructure of the Uinkaret, of the machines and binary digital instructions which animated them, was only a logic exercise he would modestly say. What he did not attempt to explain to those that admired him from other fields, was that the great complexity of, and the creativity required to manage simultaneous linear equations of music, and the creative ability to manage them, was a function of logarithmic complexity. In order to handle the simultaneous interaction of dozens, or hundreds, or thousands of linear equations, each dependent on the webbed interaction among them, was what in earlier centuries was known as the interaction of quantum mechanics. It was an application developed from an example of nature's cryptochromes, the light sensitive proteins found in the human retina and those of certain plants and in other animals. The quantum pairing of chemical radical pairs that spin in a momentary synchrony in the presence of light, allowed the perception and response to electromagnetic field, and enabled flying insects and species of bats to navigate.

"It is not enough to feed, clothe, and provide safety and shelter to the colonists being sent to Mars," he had said many times to his friend Humboldt Noraxton, though it always took his friend a moment's reflection to consider this pronouncement.

After a thoughtful pause, his friend Rotfach Theoretrics continued.

"No, it is not enough, even though I am the primary technologist focusing on everything else in the new colony's environment, except the arts."

"The beauty of your mind is not limited to mechanics and engineering," Humboldt said, waiting another moment for his friend to continue.

"But I know this now, and I have known this subconsciously since childhood, when music first spoke to the unconscious mind of my childhood, and made me feel connected to something larger than myself," replied Rotfach.

"Funny, isn't it, that my own childhood recollections are of science, and the most wonderful gift that I ever received was a microscope when I was a small child," said Humboldt.

"Yes," responded Rotfach, "our childhood dreams remain inside us as a comfort if we have been able to connect to our true life's work with love."

"There are many talents and abilities I possess which allow me to perform scientific and technological work," he continued, "arguably at a higher level than most colleagues with whom I have worked as an adult. But that is in the science and technical sphere of my chosen profession. Though my dalliance with the arts and music in particular is truly heartfelt, it is generally only heartfelt for me, as my level of skill and the ability to interpret the feelings of composers are not, and never will be, at a level required for public performance."

What Rotfach Theoretrics left unsaid were thoughts of verse and prose which only he knew existed in journals and notebooks that he had kept since he was a very young man. Willing to share his scratching attempts at music, the scribbled musings and poetry of his innermost thoughts were kept for himself alone.

"When I attempt to make music, it is thankfully, only for myself and a few close friends!" he concluded.

His oldest friend, Humboldt, nodded in appreciation of what had been expressed to him on this, and many other subjects with which they had shared over the many years of their friendship. Participation in the making of, or only participating in the enjoyment as a consumer of the arts made no matter. It was the feeling of connectedness with which one came away. A feeling of timelessness. A feeling which in the earlier centuries of ancient man might have been described as religiosity. In the matter of performance arts, with the exception of recordings, there is nothing made that lasts. And amidst all of the activity to produce real infrastructure in which it would be possible to live and breathe, the effervescence of the performance arts must be more important than the bricks and mortar in which they are performed, experienced, and enjoyed if in only a brief pause from the daily work in which mankind must continue to toil. Absent the arts, perhaps there would be no bricks and mortar in which it could be performed.

It was now possible to render all physical comforts with the power of technology. With the life-lengthening genetic alteration, people were now able to experience more than just one effective lifetime. In fact, the lengthening of lives allowed successive periods in one's life, any one of which would have previously sufficed as one full life to live. Though there was a longing in both of the old friends, Rotfach and Humboldt, that wished it could be their destiny to help create the new world of Haven and participate themselves not just in the planning and execution of the migration, but to be there at what would eventually be the permanent settlement at Lake Aeolis to begin life anew. It was a natural desire to want to take their places there with the colonists to create the new world, to be not just one of the fathers or mothers in spirit of Haven, but one of the daughters or sons on the surface of the new planet, to begin again, new, and live out the full measure of their lives, never again to return to Earth's Uinkaret. But it was their destiny to remain on Earth and see to the successful transition to Haven, and to accept an uncertain fate, not knowing the hour or the day or the year or the century when the Uinkaret might be no more. It had been their hope that Project ARK would be a colonization effort to extend humankinds dominion to an interplanetary domain. It had been their hope that for the rest of their lives and beyond for generations to come, Project Haven would not be known on the new planet only as the escape to Mars and the survival of the species of man, but as the extension of humankind's dream from a still extant Earth, of an eternal dominion over the heavens.

ix

Virtual Neutrino Wave Sensors had been launched from planet Earth to Mars, to provide a holographic monitoring of the entire Martian surface for protection from incoming space debris and remnants of comets piercing the solar system from distant stars or rogue asteroids. The bumping and colliding remnants of the nearly four-billion-year-old formation of the solar system orbited chaotically in the belt between the fourth and fifth planets. And within the asteroid belt certain singular satellites coursed in a retrograde direction to the great masses of materials – a rocky collection which, a mystery still, had never coalesced to form a planet. The Wave Sensors was a system which had, for dozens of centuries earlier, been deployed on Earth, a defense against the knowledge that extinction events of the past would inevitably occur again, incoming destruction caused by intraheliospheric or even interstellar objects. It was a system of tragic irony whose future could not have been imagined, and the knowledge of which would be forgotten, and then rediscovered to enable the survival of mankind in a way which was never intended.

Eight sensors from pole to pole at each forty-five degrees of latitude, and at each forty-five degrees of longitude – sixty-four geosynchronous virtual satellite sensors in orbit above the

Martian surface, scanning interplanetary space for the protection of the planet below. Virtual reality sensors which had the capability of unleashing real ex-atmospheric robotic peace drone projectiles against incoming comets or asteroids of the kind which had caused cataclysmic extinction events during the planetary history of three and one-half billion years on Earth.

An extinction event was never to happen again, on Earth or now on Mars, for the Uinkaret's technology had progressed to the point where an external extinction event was theoretically no longer possible. That, with the level of humankind's progression, from the development that had taken place over the last one hundred centuries, it was unthinkable that all could be destroyed, that an extinction event could erase one hundred centuries of uninterrupted development which had given man one thousand years of life instead of one hundred, and a sustainable dominion over the Earth. Not even the least among the residents of the Uinkaret wanted a return to the previous life before the science of genetics had unleashed the secrets of prolonged life. One lifetime had become an adventure of many lifetimes, to those who were not afraid to live them.

To the privileged and successful inhabitants of the Uinkaret, it was unthinkable to return to the old ways. For the Haven colony, it was a system of primary importance, a gift of life protection from Earth's Uinkaret to the inhabitants of Mars, whose technology would not be capable of producing such a protection system for generations to come, a protection which would last until the new planet's development could provide its own even more advanced technological shield from the inevitable dangers of interplanetary and interstellar space debris.

For hundreds of years these silent sentinels – scanning at an altitude of more than three times the diameter of the Earth – had fallen endlessly in their orbits around the Earth, each generation more capable of seeing into the interplanetary and ex-heliospheric realm of space beyond the Earth, peering into space, sweeping the heavens for any asteroid or comet that might have the potential to collide with Earth or its moon. Now these sentinels would do the same for their sister planet, the third blue orb, and its two tiny moons, the fourth planet from the sun of the solar system.

For one thousand eight hundred centuries, humankind would walk and attempt to develop the planet to which they had been sent to colonize from Earth. But it was not a linear development, and after the Earth's Uinkaret was destroyed before the first generation on Mars had acclimatized themselves to the new planet, there began the gradual loss of the technologies which had been initially transplanted to Haven. Before all of the flights of cargo and colonists had been launched from Earth, there was a massive release of energy from the vulcanism which had underlain the Earth's primary human settlement. The collapsing geologic underpinning of the Uinkaret gave way, and there followed a control loss of the orbital Neutrino Wave Sensors. As if choreographed in a perfect sequence, incoming space debris, small remnants of the Baptistina asteroid which had orbited chaotically after a collision within the asteroid belt 160 million years earlier, could not be managed by the Robotic Peace Drones after the control loss of the Wave Sensors, and remnants of the asteroid made their way through the atmosphere to complete a catastrophic near-human extinction event. The world on Earth that advanced mankind had known, ceased to exist. Several ships, still on their mission to Mars would arrive at the Lake surface after guidance signals from Earth no longer monitored them, but they managed to arrive safely to the colony of Haven. The tragedy of their now certain one-way journey was known before they landed on what was now the only advanced inhabitable human world, planet Mars. After the going away of one world, it was now the singular home of another. Only the far flung primitive human settlements continued their existence on Earth, the ones whom had refused to acquiesce to the demands of the Uinkaret consolidation, survived. The history of the surviving settlements would devolve once again to a prehistoric existence.

At the ARK, energy sources were established, mining resources had identified the ores required for the technology of metals, ceramics, and materials of more basic need – medical, architectural, industrial – but these had only been discovered with future potential. The mining infrastructures were not fully developed, and though the knowledge of their acquisition and use was documented in the plans for the new colony, the infrastructure was not yet sufficiently developed for its sustainable use.

Agricultural need was recognized as the first priority. The need to feed and clothe was the most basic provision for the necessity of sustainable survival of an advanced – if now a technologically and materialistically impoverished – society. The ability to access the genetic archives would be lost for generations, until the machine read capability would be reinvented once again in the very distant future. And in an ironic reversal, as man's technological stature reduced his ability to sustain the many man-made necessities which he had taken for granted on Earth, and which had been initially exported to Haven, his physical presence grew large in the one-third gravity of Mars. Successive generations physically acclimatized to the new, lower gravity environment. Physical giants would roam the surface of Mars. It would take almost two thousand centuries for the level of society on Mars to once again match the larger presence of their physical beings.

X

Mars Colony One was established on the broad plain bordering Lake Aeolis which filled the volcanic depression from which the mountain rose, and once established, the early explorers tasked themselves with a permanent structure located within the mountain itself, within the security of the inner self-sealing doors and behind the air locked entrance, protected by the external GCDs. This heavily fortified structure became the nerve center of the expanding settlements which eventually colonized almost all areas of the planet with the exception of the two frozen polar regions which had yielded themselves only to scientific exploration.

For one thousand eight hundred centuries man colonized the new world. The ARK of Haven, and the DNA record of all Earth life had survived the interplanetary journey to Mars where mankind was destined to continue what was to be the eternal life and necessary intragalactic survival in the inevitable exhaustion of the solar system. But now, life on this planet, too, was about to come to an end.

The site of the first Mars settlement complex was one of the last areas to be obliterated. It was one of the few areas not targeted by a senseless attack from one of the multiple independently directed robotic peace drones, the enforcement vehicles of the Constant Surveillance Machines. The purpose of these CSMs had been to scan the heavens for potentially destructive space debris from their positions in virtual near Mars orbit, a lasting protection, the last gift of survival which had been launched from Earth in the midst of the colonization of Haven. The system had survived long enough so that humankind's survival was thought to be ensured once again on man's second planet.

The first seismic detections were received at the mountain which rose five kilometers from the depths of the freshwater lake in which it stood. The Genetic Containment Doors on Aeolis Mons were automatically sealed. But it was a false seismic detection. It was instead the concussion of the first nuclear detonation caused by a misdirected CSM peace drone. In the cascading event which followed, responding drones would complete the destruction of the surface of the planet.

Exploratory flights back to Earth had brought crews of the long-lived giants of Mars to their former home. What was found by these returning Earth explorers was what had been lost one hundred eighty thousand years before – the remnants of tribes abandoned on continents far from the destruction of the Uinkaret – and then these tribes too, had been lost to history. All that remained was the indecipherable hieroglyphics carved into the Earth at various far-flung areas on the Earth's surface, beckoning the returners from space.

Now these giants from the Mars new world were marooned on the old Earth world, unprepared, and unable to return to Mars where the ARK of Haven no longer existed, abandoned onto the old world where written language had been forgotten, and the old languages had receded into a babble of cacophonies.

Great masses of the Mars atmosphere ejected into space propelled by the heat of a million suns, molecules boiled to incandescence, then transmutation and escape velocity, a cascading effect which consumed nearly two quadrillion kilotons of an atmosphere no longer pressed against the surface of the planet. Hurricane forces of plasma and plasticized tornado vortexes scoured the invisible, odorless, tasteless gases from every surface, as whole valleys which had been ejected to near space returned, now incandescent, through the roaring atmosphere to burn what remained on the surface with infrared radiance. Animate life had already abandoned, and all that remained perished as the world and ninety-eight percent of the atmosphere vanished. Glaciers simply ceased to exist, releasing their ancient ice to be melted and liquified in a momentary torrent or directly sublimated in a more violent outgassing, bypassing the liquid phase in a near instantaneous destruction. Great plains emerged from the depths, seas swept away in a superheated cauldron, while the mountainous regions of Coprates, Tyrrhenum, and Nachos remained broken and buckled under the concussive effects of the accumulating pressures. Both mountains and ocean plains arose, no longer pressed to the surface by the pressure of the waters weight or the disappearing atmosphere. All moisture and evidence of life succumbed. The shining star that had been the sun in the sky vanished against the logarithmic illumination of the atmosphere, and had already blinded, before it destroyed, any life that had turned in its direction for the last time to sense its warmth and comfort and then lose the source of life and energy in a death so instantaneous that the sensing of its loss itself was lost.

Almost two thousand centuries of man and beast and billions of years of oceanic and terrestrial outgassing vanished from the surface and atmosphere as effortlessly from the third blue orb as if there had been a dozen or millions of lost centuries. An extinction event across which its event horizon swallowed all that had been wrought and all that would be lost. The atmosphere was replaced by silence broken only by the periodic winds that were generated by the unmoderated vacillations of modest daytime warmth versus bitter nighttime temperatures.

What had been destroyed was now abandoned, cooled through ages of geologic history, and for two hundred thousand years, charged atoms of the remaining atmosphere escaped while the solar wind stripped what was left of atmospheric molecules in a constant passionless, emotionless, uninhabited dissipation, and an additional quadrillion kilograms of its thinning atmosphere vanished into the clouds of interplanetary post-solar debris. All that remained was a fine and final dust, and the impact craters buried beneath.

Were the particle impacts of the solar wind against the surface amplified a million times, as if it were possible to hear a beating human heart, silence would only be met with silence. A rumbling imperceptible bass of drumbeats and silent regret, without hope of a rescuing discovery.

For two hundred millenniums the remaining winds blew across the face of the planet, lifeless dissolution and endless particulate storms, awaiting the return to the planet, which would in time, bleed to red.

V
541 Return

i

Morning, Cape Canaveral Air Force Station, partly cloudy 75 degrees with light winds aloft, November 26, 2011, Launch Complex 41.

The tree of life had been planted on Mars almost two hundred thousand years ago. The population and colonization of the planet took place by the ingenuity of our species, and then the great nuclear extinction event happened, such an event this time by the hand of man himself. It was not like nature's Caldera Catastrophe which had destroyed the Quaternary Uinkaret here on Earth, leaving no trace of that earlier civilization which vanished from the face of the Earth four thousand centuries earlier, now buried deep below the surface of the Earth, encased first by pyroclastic tephra, then the lava flows of the Caldera. But unlike the first interplanetary migration from Earth's Uinkaret to the ARK, there had been no time to plan an orderly return from Mars to Earth, and the desperate launches from a Mars in the midst of destruction that were able to be completed almost 200,000 years ago, would result in the last known rise of homo sapiens from the landing sites in the northern regions of the southern continents. Earlier flights to other regions of the Earth had only been technological outposts sent to reconnoiter regions of all the continents. These were abandoned, those few individuals who were marooned there were left to fend for themselves, sometimes marking locations massive enough with rudimentary structures to be seen from Earth orbit in the hope of rescue and return to Mars. But the conflagration of their Mars homeland was visible to a discerning eye, and what was once a shimmering blue orb, became a harbinger of death and destruction of a world to which they would never be able to return.

Instead, over the millenniums it turned to a rust-red pinprick in the sky, no longer a shimmering blue beneath its lost atmosphere and oceans. Those few who had returned to Earth knew of no survivors on Mars, and there was no communication possible between the few survivors who had returned to Earth's great southern continent and those remaining ancients in the lost regions of the other continents. All remaining survivors from Earth's previous world lived and died alone, leaving few known scratches on the surface of the Earth. These were yet to be discovered, withered and worn over the previous two thousand centuries of time and loss. The surviving descendants of the returned explorers from Mars no longer grew to the stature of their ancestors, and their eight hundred or nine hundred or one thousand years of life reverted again to a nature limited – an evolutionary nature – of only one hundred years, and for almost all individuals many years less in a cruel natural world without the genetic technology inherited from an earlier Earth, and known for two hundred thousand years on Mars.

The child no longer knew its mother.

Both physical stature and intellectual learning would be lost in the southern continent wildernesses, to which man now returned. Everything had been lost which had been carried for the previous two hundred thousand years of life spanning two planets. Time would turn again for another two thousand centuries on Earth, until once again science and technology was rediscovered which enabled mankind to reach above the surface of the Earth to the heavens. The knowledge of man's previous journeys would remain undiscovered and as unknowable as messages in the strands of DNA which survived to tell its story, still as unreadable and incapable of being retrieved and understood as the data which continued to orbit inside the ancient spacecraft which still maintained its eternal journey around the sun, between the seventh and eighth planets. A compendium of life and what it was before humankind's journey to the fourth planet after the destruction of Earth's home, followed by the destruction of Mars, and the tragic return again to Earth. Two hundred thousand years ago there was no triumphant entry along an Appian Way, to a capital city awaiting the spoils of a returning army.

ii

Standing fifty-eight meters (nineteen stories) tall, weighing five hundred thirty-one thousand kilograms, an Atlas V-541 ELV rocket. This Expendable Launch Vehicle, with a five-meter payload fairing nose cone, four solid-rocket boosters around a RD-180 central booster core, and a Centaur upper stage with one RL-10A engine, stood ready to launch at 15:02 GMT, for a journey through interplanetary space which was to take two hundred fifty-four days. All of this mass, all to carry only 0.17% of the total mass of the launch vehicle to the surface of a planet, a delivery of less than nine hundred kilograms, to place the Mars Rover Curiosity at the base of Mount Sharp inside Gale Crater.

Main engine start at T-minus one second, main engine ignition, and solid rocket boosters ignited.

Liftoff.

Within ten seconds of the beginning of the ascent, the Atlas V rocket had already risen 900 meters above the surface of the Earth. Within a few moments of time, it had already risen above the height of the highest man-made structure on Earth, and began the arc of its flight.

In forty seconds, heading east out over the Atlantic Ocean, the Atlas V launch vehicle throttled back to seventy-six percent thrust and it broke through the sound barrier, three hundred forty-three meters per second, as the rocket booster chamber pressures tracked on a nominal curve, illuminated on the screen of one of the NASA launch control engineers.

Counting fifty seconds, the vehicle passed through max Q, the maximum dynamic pressure which impacted the spacecraft like a jackhammer, pulsating and pushing and forcing the accelerating craft through the fluid dynamics of the Earth's thinning atmosphere, still viscous at the temperature and pressure of its speed, impacting violently against the vehicle approaching to the limit of its design strength.

At plus one minute into the flight, the center main RD-180 engine throttled up to one hundred percent with pressure readings nominal, and flight control disturbances as expected. The craft flew on until ninety seconds into the flight.

Then burnout of the SRB's, and the solid rocket boosters jettison away from the spacecraft.

First pair jettisoned.

Second pair jettisoned.

Both pairs fall safely away from the vehicle, tumbling to a splash down into the Atlantic Ocean where they settled to the bottom, expended, their less than two-minute lifespan complete.

Freed of the booster engines, guidance re-enabled. All readings nominal at two minutes into the flight. Pushed forward by the thrust of the center main engine alone, the craft is now thirty-two nautical miles in altitude, fifty-four miles downrange, traveling at seventy-nine hundred kilometers per hour. The turbulence of the thin Mesospheric atmosphere is no longer a factor against the spacecraft's upper stage Centaur rocket, or the rover assembly payload tucked safely beneath the payload fairing. The engines throttle back to hold a constant 2.5G level, the maximum pressure possible to safely accommodate the jettison of the protective fairing.

The world in view of the spacecraft now becomes separated into two sharply distinct parts; the blackness of space above, and the blue-white curve of the Earth below. There are no shadows to be perceived here. There is no transition to light versus darkness.

A pyro valve fires to pressurize the Centaur's Reaction Control System to allow thruster navigation adjustments in its journey through space, burning brightly against the blackness of space around it, creating an incandescent glow between the Earth and space which illuminated the central booster core. The pressure increases in the loop as expected. All readings, nominal.

Three minutes post liftoff, on the 2.5G curve limit, coming up on payload fairing jettison. The graphite epoxy sheets of the fairing, stiffened by their aluminum honeycomb cores, have protected the rocket's payload from the turbulence of the rapidly dissipating atmosphere. Now the stress of the explosive release bolts causes the panels to bow and flex like thin flexible plastic shrouds as gravity claims them. They, and the Centaur's forward load reactor disk, which had kept the panels firmly positioned against the skin of the rocket and payload, are no longer needed. The payload fairings and reactor disk tumble through the upper atmosphere to also find their resting place in the Atlantic, which has already claimed the four spent rocket boosters.

As the craft surges forward, a barely visible smudge of carbon along a trailing edge of the jettisoned fairing is all that remains of a tiny Drosophila melanogaster that had flown into a crevice between the booster stage and the Centaur engine, and nested in the morning before liftoff. The DNA of this tiny creature contained four pairs of chromosomes and one hundred sixty-five million base pairs of AC-TG nucleotides which had been held together by hydrogen bonds. The craft, directed by only four million lines of computer code by comparison, discarded this bit of carbon to be consumed in its fiery return to Earth along with the jettisoned boosters and payload fairing.

Finally, the last remaining throttle up of the RD-180 main engine pushes the Atlas V booster to eighty-nine percent thrust, at a constant 4.6G acceleration. At four minutes from launch, the booster phase chill down sequence begins, with engine housing temperatures responding in preparation for booster engine cut off.

We have BECO and stage separation.

The massive first stage Atlas V rocket tumbles away and falls to Earth, to be subsumed into the waters of the Atlantic.

Fuel prestart for the upper stage Centaur, ignition, and full thrust of the RL-10A engine. The spacecraft rotates ninety degrees. Where the blue tinted whiteness and the curvature of the Earth was, now is the blackness of space, and the visible pinpricks of stars.

Steering enabled.

A four hundred sixty-two second Centaur first burn is complete, and MECO.

The main engine cut off silences the spacecraft, and it is parked into a low Earth orbit to begin its coast period, still captured in the free fall gravity of Earth.

Coasting complete.

A four hundred seventy second trans-planetary injection burn of the RL-10A Centaur engine moves the spacecraft beyond the one hundred sixty-five-kilometer perihelion of Earth orbit. It now slingshots to Mars at ten thousand four hundred kilometers per hour as guidance calculated commands move the spacecraft into the proper trajectory. The flight control computer orders four pyrotechnic bolts to fire and free MSL from Centaur. At the same time, the spent second stage Centaur rocket performs an avoidance maneuver that takes it out of the flight path, and the Deep Space Network acquires the signal for Mission Control, Houston.

The Mars Science Laboratory begins its journey to Mars, released from the Launch Vehicle Adapter that connected the cruise stage to the two rocket engines that had brought it first to Earth orbit, then on to interplanetary space.

Slowly spinning at two revolutions per minute, the four-meter diameter cruise stage stabilizes the forward momentum of MSL. It rotates around the central axis of the machined aluminum internal structure which supports the spacecraft, much like the endoskeletal support of the men and women who made her.

Guided by the heavens, a star scanner monitors the cruise stage's position relative to the 360° three-dimensional star field of our Milky Way galaxy in which it flies. There are four trajectory course corrections scheduled along the way, powered by eight hydrazine fueled thrusters fed from twin titanium tanks. The cruise stage will monitor and control the temperature and operating conditions of the spacecraft via the rover's flight control computer. Heat will be both dissipated and retained for the spacecraft, with pumps and fluids circulated through the radiator of the Heat Rejection System, and through the use of insulating materials to keep instruments warmer than the less than liquid nitrogen temperatures of interplanetary space through which it will fly through the heavens beyond its Earth.

iii

For two hundred nine days the Cruise Phase continues while the onboard rover flight control computer monitors all systems of the spacecraft, and then transfers the data to the cruise stage for X band transmissions to mission control. A forty-five-day Approach Phase follows with extensive trajectory control maneuvers, vehicle checkouts, and subsystem monitoring and calibration. Final navigation data is transmitted to the Mars Science Laboratory from Mission Control Houston as MSL approaches planet Mars.

EDL phase – Entry, Descent, and Landing – with its five hundred ten thousand lines of computer code, begins at Mars entry minus 5 days. Monitoring by the Deep Space Network Coverage increases with critical navigation data streaming to and from the approaching spacecraft. Doppler tracking and Delta Differential One-Way Ranging measurements using the 34-meter and 70-meter Deep Space Network antennae determine the orbit and then calculate the Entry Interface Point requirement in order to intercept the precise MSL landing site at Gale Crater. Three Trajectory Correction Maneuvers adjust the vehicle's path to the correct EIP. The first is a planned engine burn at entry minus 2 days. Number two and number three TCM burns occur at Entry minus 1 day, and Entry minus 9 hours.

Two hours and 33,500 kilometers from the Gale Crater landing site, now moving at 4,000 meters per second, the final navigation update from controllers on Earth is received by MSL with an estimation of where the spacecraft's precise position will be at nine minutes to Entry Interface with the Martian atmosphere. From now on, two hours before landing, the MSL will fly using this final human command, and from this moment until the surface landing, the MSL flight computers will utilize their own navigation sensors and internal measurement units to determine the real time flight sequence maneuvers necessary until radar data about the planet's surface is activated after heat shield jettison. But that is yet to come, and much must take place in near perfect sequence in the next one hundred and thirteen minutes before Atmospheric Entry and the final seven minutes to touchdown, during which the MSL's automatic landing sequence must independently guide the craft safely to the surface.

In thirty minutes, MSL crosses the orbit of the Martian moon Deimos, and in one more hour it will cross the orbital path of Phobos, traversing the path of both Martian moons.

Exo-Atmospheric Entry begins at EI-15 minutes, when the Flight Control System issues the "Do EDL Entry Mode" command to the MSL flight computer, and initiates the transition from Pre-EDL to EDL – the Entry, Descent and Landing sequence. After 90 seconds, the cruise stage Heat Rejection System is vented a final three minutes, the interplanetary monitoring of heating and cooling for the last two hundred fifty-four days is now complete.

Distance to Gale Crater:	5,216 kilometers
Altitude:	2,820 kilometers
Velocity:	5.1 kilometers/sec
Entry Interface:	EI-14:06 minutes

Distance to Horizon: 3,557 kilometers

Mars MSL approaches the red planet, crossing over the border between Arabia, Syrtis Major, and Iapygia. It is passing from darkness to light, with the sun at the horizon ahead of it, descending to its atmospheric entry during which the surface of its heat shield will glow white with a temperature equal to that of the surface of the sun. The distance to the curving horizon turning beneath it in the eastern direction of flight is 3,557 kilometers, while the northern to southern horizon visible to the port and the starboard of the spacecraft spans nearly 7,000 kilometers – the nearly full diameter of the planet is visible to the onrushing craft. The atmosphere's dusty haze reaches only one hundred and twenty-five kilometers into space, a thickness of only 2% above the surface of the planet within the expanse of view, almost insignificant and easily missed as the craters and gullies, ravines and mountains, and cruel slashes through the boron intubated crust begin to appear and would catch your view. It is a view which you would see were the spacecraft a living, breathing, seeing presence. But the atmosphere is only a thin veil over the ruddy terrain, a fragile wisp rising from the surface, thin as a bird's wing, like the remembrance of a risen sorrow, a reflection of what was once on and above the surface, vanishing to space, a resurrection to nothingness, a redemption forgotten and abandoned, the harbinger of pitiless centuries to come and those which have passed, and the red planet's fitting symbol of war to those that made the machine over which its surface it now flies.

At EI-10 minutes, ten pyrotechnic bolts cut the cables which fastened the cruise stage to the rover descent module's protective back aeroshell, and the cruise stage separates. The MSL Entry, Descent and Landing Instrument suite activates. The sensors and electronics of the EDLI package will measure the atmospheric entry and heat shield performance during the Mars landing sequences. This new MEDLI data, never before experienced or captured on a craft as large as MSL, will assist in the design parameter requirements of the entry shields for future Mars missions. The jettisoned cruise stage is diverted into a trajectory moving safely away from the rover's module, to burn up in the Martian atmosphere, its function complete, the remains of which will be vaporized completely, 4,000 kilometers behind the rover's targeted landing site at Gale Crater.

EDL communication is activated. From now until landing, the spacecraft will communicate directly with NASA Jet Propulsion Laboratory Mission Control using X band Tomes indicating nominal or off-nominal performance on a one-way transmission. An 8kbps UHF antennae will also transmit its signal to the Odyssey spacecraft orbiting above MSL which in turn will relay the signal transmitted to Earth. Both communications will be sent with a Mars send and Earth receive delay of 13 minutes and 51 seconds, crossing the distance from MSL to NASA of 249 million kilometers. By the time Curiosity has landed or crashed, almost 14 minutes will have passed before the information is received by ground control on Earth.

Three Mars reconnaissance orbiters will monitor and witness the landing of the spacecraft; NASA's Mars Reconnaissance Orbiter, NASA's Mars Odyssey Orbiter, and the European Space Agency's Mars Express.

Distance to target:	3,971 kilometers
Altitude:	2,045 kilometers
Velocity:	5.2 kilometers/second
Entry Interface:	EI-10:00 minutes
Distance to Horizon:	2,668 kilometers

"We are seeing RCS warm-up."
"Curiosity is reporting."

In one additional minute, the descent module Reaction Control System is activated. Consisting of 8 thrusters in 4 double ports, it will control the spacecraft's orientation from de-spin through powered descent, backshell separation, and flyaway. The descent module, consisting of the backshell and heat shield within which is housed the descent stage and rover, de-spins from two rotations per minute to zero rpm in a maneuver lasting three minutes, cancelling out the spin which has stabilized the craft during its interplanetary voyage from Earth.

Distance to target:	3,336 kilometers
Altitude:	1,565 kilometers
Velocity:	5.2 kilometers/second
Entry Interface:	EI- 08:00 minutes
Distance to Horizon:	2,267 kilometers

Through the atmospheric haze, a subtle reddish glow now emanates from the surface below. The approaching spacecraft is no longer stabilized by its rotating motion, the movement of which has been slowed then stopped by the RCS backshell jets in preparation for impending entry. Now the exposed and vulnerable craft is balanced precariously without the rotational stabilization of its spin. Its orientation to the surface and toward its target landing site will now depend on powered telemetric navigation, first using the eight hydrazine fueled thrusters on the backshell, and later, during landing, the additional eight engines of the Descent Stage. Still, only major geographic features are visible on the planet of the rapidly approaching surface below. Valleys and craters and plains gradually begin to appear out of the albedo features of Mars, which are apparent when viewed from a distance. Now at closer range, the surface features appear like the identifying visage of a human face, viewed at a close enough distance where recognition is capable for identification out of the long-distance chaos of a crowd.

The craft overflies Arabia, leaving Terra Sabaea and the ancient river valley, the Naktong Vallis, behind, crosses the Janssen impact crater with its violently breached outer wall, the southeast breach of which marks a catastrophic unknown remembrance which vanished before it was recorded. Now entering Syrtis Major, and skirting its southern border, there are views northeast over that province and southwest over Iapygia which borders it to the south. In a few minutes the craft's heat shield will interact with an atmosphere one hundred times less dense than that of Earth's, but which will still provide enough aerodynamic drag at the speed and mass of the spacecraft to produce temperatures equal to those on the surface of the sun, blinding any possible views to the planet below while the surface of its heat shield glows incandescent. Now, after the silent journey from within the blackness of interplanetary space, the craft flies at Mach 15, gathering additional speed as it is drawn into the increasing gravitational force. The blackness of space has been replaced by the ruddy planet's surface slowly revolving beneath it. The spacecraft is overflying craters, mountains, ancient volcanoes, moraine deposits, and lost seas boiled or sublimated to nothingness – while over all of it lies a surface scarred by violence and worn by dust clouds over the ages, a universal cycle of destruction, redemption, and destruction, breaths of a universe witnessed by the robotic traveler built by the beings who have not yet been enabled to return to see what their machines have already witnessed long before this arrival.

A backward glance would see the free falling 400kilogram cruise stage, still spinning at two revolutions per minute, dip into the atmosphere at one hundred twenty-five kilometers above the surface. It is an aluminum structured donut shape which has shepherded the spacecraft on its flight from Earth, monitoring communications and guidance, providing thermal protection, and covered by the solar cells that provided a continuous charge to the batteries which in turn powered the craft. It navigated its journey by the stars like the earliest explorers that sailed across the oceans above which it flew as it left the Earth and her orbit. The journey to the nearest planet would take as long as did the first sailing ships to cross the ocean over which it flew when it left the bounds of Earth's gravity, and would travel a distance ninety thousand times greater than the wooden boats of the first intercontinental explorers. Detached from its charge, the spent cruise stage begins to roll backwards, and falls ever-so-full-of-grace like the movement of a dancer, before its movements become wild and uncontrolled as it falls on toward the surface of the planet which it will never impact, to engage the atmosphere in an uncontrolled roll now that its eight hydrazine guidance thrusters are no longer operable from the twin titanium tanks that had seeded their power. The solar cells and antennae units which had been secured to its surface peel off violently, claimed by the friction against the upper atmosphere and are gone, and its aluminum structure will begin to glow, then melt and be torn apart, then vaporized in brilliant flashes that will descend through the atmosphere, a sublime burning up which will not reach and will not rest upon the dust of the planet's surface. Its mission done, its presence cremated, vaporized, will mix within what is left of the thinned atmosphere of lost millenniums. Dust to dust as in all things.

In preparation for entry into the Martian atmosphere, two 75kilogram tungsten external cruise stage balance masses are explosively jettisoned from the back of the aeroshell. Now the craft, no longer balanced along the spin axis of the interplanetary cruise phase, dips eighteen degrees from its longitudinal axis in thirty seconds, increasing the lift to drag ratio of the craft, providing enough lift for telemetric guided maneuvers necessary for a controlled atmospheric entry. The angle of attack through the Martian atmosphere must remain within sixteen to twenty degrees. Preprogrammed data is no longer used to fly the descending craft. Real time data is now processed by the onboard MSL computers to generate navigational responses. Prior to performing the landing maneuvers, the spacecraft enters a five-minute Quiescent Period during which time it rapidly increases its velocity with the pull of the planet's gravity beneath it. During this time, it must acquire enough data to calibrate two Inertial Measurement Units which will be the source of the landing navigation data when Atmospheric Entry begins.

Surface features are now seen clearly. The field of view extends two thousand kilometers from port to starboard. Within the thousand-kilometer view ahead of the spacecraft, Gale Crater appears halfway to the horizon, though it is still too distant to perceive the height of the six-kilometer-high Aeolis Mons, Mount Sharp, rising out of the depths of the crater. We are crossing the northern border of Tyrrhenum now, east of Escalante, still northwest of Robert Sharp, leaving the Amenthes Quadrangle's great Terra Cimmeria, to skirt the northeast corner of Tyrrhenum and enter the northwest tip of Aeolis.

"Vehicle is reporting it has completed its turn to entry and spin down"

"Cruise balance masses separated."

"Vehicle is sending heartbeat tomes, should be quiet for the next several minutes."

"We are about seven minutes to entry."

"We are now five minutes to entry."

"OD227 run out looks like a missed distance of 232 meters, over."

"Less than divert."

"Roger."

"Two minutes to entry."

"Thirty seconds to entry."

"Vehicle reports entry interface."

"Distance to target 678 kilometers."

"Altitude from Base of Gale Crater 131 kilometers."

"Velocity 5.9 kilometers per second."

At Entry Interface EI-00:00, at a distance to horizon of 700 kilometers, tracking data for Orbital Determination from the Deep Space Network's two-way range and doppler data is used to make delta differential one-way range measurements on two baselines, along with the on-craft camera optical approach navigation data. The position and velocity must be determined at the targeted radial distance from the center of Mars, a distance of 3,522.2 kilometers and an altitude of 125 kilometers from the surface at the point of entry. At this atmospheric entry position, the Entry, Descent, and Landing programming commits the spacecraft to enter the Martian atmosphere. Following the commands programmed into the EDL coding suite, Entry has begun, and the spacecraft having shed its cruise stage, begins the final stage of its journey to the surface of Mars from the surface of Earth, from which it was launched nearly a year earlier.

Mountains are now clearly in view below the craft which begins to sense the drag of the heat shield on the increasingly dense atmosphere, still an atmosphere so slight that it is only the craft's hyperspeed that creates the sensation of an atmospheric push back. Now, before the blindness induced by the enveloping incandescence of the heat shield overwhelms its outward view, we can determine the mountains and plateaus of the crater Bober Sharp, having passed Graben Troughs first to the west, and then to the north of the western crater rim. Extreme geologic violence caused these ancient faults in the surface; a cauldron of molten rock had risen up to the surface where waters once collected from melting glaciers, vanished, sublimated, leaving the gashes in the surface over which the craft now flies before its own incandescent blinding re-entry.

Other surface features appear – the lines of ridges of claylike materials, high-fired ceramics left to form gates and walls creating channels on the surface as the softer materials which were violently heaped up about them, eroded away, forming layered deposits, the kind of which would be studied on the most intensive scale at Gale Crater.

Were there eyes to see beyond the protection of the heat shield, this would be the first panoramic view of the now red planet, as the craft dips closer to the surface than any of the three orbiting spacecraft circling above the planet, and helping to monitor the flight of MSL.

iv

The genetic code of every living organism is contained in the base pair nucleotides of DNA, divided into the linear molecules of the chromosomes. It is the DNA genetic code which commands the messenger RNA to copy and carry it from the cell nucleus to the cytoplasm where proteins are assembled from amino acids. In much the same way, the four million lines of code embedded in the flash memory of Curiosity's computer directs the CPU to perform all the flight sequences from lift-off to the landing not yet accomplished. But the spacecraft flies with only one one-millionth of the codes compared to the codes required for those that comprise the human genetic sequence of 46 chromosomes in 23 pairs.

At zero second countdown to landing, the mission's seven-minute descent phase sequence has begun.

On the two hundred fifty-fifth day of its mission, the spacecraft interacts with the Martian world for the first time, touched by the 95% carbon dioxide molecules in the atmosphere of its new destiny, still directed by only one-fortieth the genetic lines of code of the tiny Drosophila melanogaster that had flown into the crevice between the booster stage and the Centaur engine where it had nested in the morning before liftoff. Its one-hundred sixty-five million base pairs of AC-TG nucleotides, held together by hydrogen bonds, were reduced to a carbon smudge, burned on the trailing edge of the ejected fairing in the fire of the Centaur engine. Any remaining traces of the burned carbon result of what it had been, would now be transformed to a few molecules of carbon dioxide, added to the Martian atmosphere through which it now flies, an incandescence shining brighter than the distant sun, its heat shield illuminating the path through which it will fly, stabilized by eight hydrazine thrusters, angled to bring its heat shield burn through to the surface. The activities of flight directed by the craft's computer codes from liftoff to surface approach, pales in complexity compared to the sophistication and capability of the tiny melanogaster sacrificed upon leaving the old world for the new.

Entry interface is detected at EDL zero seconds. Four monomethylhydrazine fuel tanks are pressurized which will fuel the eight backshell thrusters of the Reaction Control System, two thrusters paired with each of the four propellant tanks. These tanks will also fuel the eight powerful Descent Stage Mars Landing Engines of the Powered Descent Vehicle, two engines also paired per each tank. Each of the four propellant tanks contain 97.5 kilograms of fuel. Nominal usage estimated at 298 kilograms for the descent engines consuming hydrazine at 4 kilograms per second, with a 20 second fuel reserve for MLE burns during the descent and sky crane flyaway.

Utilizing its eight RCS thrusters, the spacecraft rotates to a descent entry attitude to present the heat shield to the entry interface with the Martian atmosphere, at an altitude of one hundred twenty-five kilometers above the surface of the planet, one hundred thirty-one kilometers above the floor of Gale Crater. Moving now at a velocity of five thousand nine hundred meters per second it will begin its final luminous plunge to the surface of the planet.

The landing ellipse is a 6x18 kilometer target within Gale Crater on the southeast side of Aeolis Mons, now only 678 kilometers in the distance. The Mons is the largest mountain within view on the surface of the planet, rising 5.5 kilometers from the valley floor of Gale Crater's one hundred fifty-four kilometers diameter. The edge of Curiosity's heat shield dips into the atmosphere towards the crater's western rim. The spacecraft is now travelling at its highest approach velocity, as gravity captures it and pulls it into the outer limits of the atmosphere. It is now traveling at almost six kilometers per second.

"We are standing by for guidance start."
"Start guided entry."
"Vehicle has reported via Tomes."

"Nominal."
"Guided entry has begun."

At the point at which MSL experiences an equivalent 0.5G force Earth load, the EDL software initiates Range Control to enable precise guiding to the Gale Crater landing site. Navigation commands are sent to the RCS thrusters for on/off correction bursts. After maintaining its preliminary entry interface angle of attack, the active Range Control Phase of supersonic entry begins using actual telemetry data in order to minimize the downrange error as MSL seeks out its targeted landing site, directed by the calculations of its onboard computers.

"Initiate Range Control Phase at 0.5 G's."
"Initiate heading alignment."
"First bank reversal started."
"Bank complete."
"We are seeing peak acceleration."

The 4.5meter diameter heat shield, constructed of large phenolic impregnated carbon ablator tiles, glows white hot as it burns through peak heating and deceleration for four minutes at up to 2,100° C, stabilized by the bursts of its hydrazine fueled RCS thrusters.

"We have passed through peak heating and acceleration."
"Reporting G's of 11 to 12 Earth G's."
"Flight GSA calling."

The General Services Administration provides electronic systems support to NASA's Jet Propulsion Laboratory, capturing and communicating data sent from MSL to Odyssey which is then relayed to GSA Earth stations.

"GSA flight, go."
"We are processing data from Odyssey."

"We are now getting telemetry from Odyssey."

"Hypersonic bank reversal 2 is starting."

"Bank reversal 2 complete."

Alternating areas of flat plains and escarpments rise out of the surface in seeming random sequence followed by areas of greater density and low mountains. The escarpments extend many linear kilometers, intersecting groups of low hills spread out like branches on the limb of a tree. Other areas of higher elevations, extending broadly underneath the spacecraft's approach, expose palisades darker than the valleys lining the randomly directional hills. Another flat plateaued region appears again with lines drawn through the flat valleys. Light and dark surfaces alternate to the horizon, and here and there an arid steppe seems to emerge beyond the valley of a circling barranca, while butte-like structures and smaller mesas, similar to those in Earth's desert southwest, break the flat surfaces extending beyond the forward, onrushing view.

The horizon of a new world plays out beyond, the darkness of space sealing the curving edge of the planet with the delicate layer of its atmosphere pillowing against the ruddy surface, the craft shaking rhythmically as it hammers through the upper atmosphere, encased within the roaring of the heat shield's incandescent radiation.

"Heading alignment phase begun."

"Error range control minus 1.2 kilometers."

"Cross range error compensated, heading for target."

"Horizontal velocity Mach 2.4, altitude 17 kilometers."

"Standby for straighten up, fly right, and parachute deploy."

"Vehicle continues to decelerate."

"We are down to Mach 2."

"As a reminder, we should have parachute deploy at about Mach 1.7."

"We are at 15 kilometers altitude."

"Stand by to begin 25kilogram balance mass ejection maneuvers."

The remaining six 25kg internal balance masses are now jettisoned by pyrotechnic release. The two 75kg external balance masses which were ejected to create the angle of attack necessary for atmospheric entry, created a center of gravity offset which must now be removed prior to deployment of the supersonic drag chute.

"Predict ejections when downrange is 1.597km."

"Sequence ejections in 2 second intervals."

"Jettison balance mass number 1."

"Jettison 2."

"Jettison 3."

"Jettison 4."

"Jettison 5."

"Jettison 6."

"EDL ops – mass ejection complete."

"Odyssey systems on EDL ops."

"180° azimuth turn complete to align Terminal Descent Sensor for ground acquisition."

"Parachute deployed."

At an Altitude of 11 kilometers, and a velocity of 450 meters per second, the 15.5meter disk chute is pyrotechnically deployed with the detonation of the largest of the 76 EDL explosive devices carried on MSL. The supersonic chute is suspended on 80 lines, 50.5 meters long. It weighs 45 kilograms, and will withstand a drag force of 30,000 kilograms, as the supersonic spacecraft is violently decelerated. In less than three minutes, the chute will slow the craft to 100 meters per second, withstanding 9Gs as it opens, preparing it for heatshield and backshell separation before the final powered descent to the surface. From its orbit around the planet high above MSL, NASA's Mars Reconnaissance Orbiter searches for, finds, and photographs Curiosity and its parachute during its supersonic descent.

"Cross range and downrange course correction."

"Range Control System guidance re-enabled."

"Thrusters have been re-enabled."

"We will control our attitude on chute."

"Roll, pitch and yaw active."

"Activate RCS torque control on chute."

"We are decelerating."

"Wrist mode RCS dynamics nominal."

"Descent vehicle oscillation acceptable."

"Transonic to subsonic velocity."

"We are at 150 meters per second."

"Dynamic phase, come back again with wrist mode dynamics."

"Wrist mode is nominal."

"Downrange net filter converge with a velocity correction of 0.7 meters per second."

"We have acquired the ground with radar at 8km altitude."

"Velocity Trigger initiated for heat shield separation and TDS activation."

"We are at 120 meters per second."

"Heat shield has separated, descent sensor nominal."

"We have found the ground."

"Standing by for backshell separation."

The 3-axis Doppler Velocimeter and Slant Range Altimeter calculates the position and movement of the craft which still consists of the supersonic chute, backshell, descent stage, and rover.

The craft descends and the Mars Descent Imager captures fixed focus full color images, five per second, documenting the descent through touchdown. The MARDI images will be stored in computer memory for communications uplink to Earth in the first few days on the planet's surface. These pictures will provide visual data on the position of MSL in Gale Crater, and will help determine the planned initial movements of the Rover.

The landing radar of the Mars Terminal Descent Sensor casts 6 Ka-band pulse doppler radar beams to the planet's surface, eight seconds after heat shield jettison and fall away. There is an allowance that only one radar beam be temporarily blocked by the cast-off heat shield. Pyrotechnic charges will next separate the backshell from the Powered Descent Vehicle. The craft will accelerate to 125meters per second after it freefalls from the backshell. After the freefall begins and until landing, the TDS will be the primary navigation sensor for MSL.

"Standing by to prime the Mars Landing Engines in preparation for powered flight."

"We are down to 90 meters per second at an altitude of 6.5 kilometers and descending."

"We are down to 86 meters per second at an altitude of 4 kilometers and descending."

"We have lost tomes to Earth at this time as expected."

"We are continuing on Odyssey telemetry."

"Ground solution equals minus 10.8 meters."

"Vertical velocity of minus 82.8 meters per second."

"Power descent start enabled."

"Signal to Odyssey is still strong."

"Pyrotechnic fuel flow initiated, engines at 1% thrust."

Descent stage and rover are primed for an 8 second freefall as all 6 pulse doppler radar beams scan the surface for the impending landing zone. Engine thrust is increased to 20%.

"Backshell and chute separation."

Pyrotechnic charges fire and the craft falls free of the chute and backshell at an altitude of less than 2 kilometers. The parachute and backshell float down to the surface a safe distance away from the landing site. Without a powered descent, the now free-falling rover would impact the surface and be lost in less than 20 seconds.

The Powered Descent Vehicle engines throttle up to 100% and freefall ends. The vehicle begins to follow the 3D trajectory mapped to the landing zone by the Ka-band doppler radar.

"We are in powered flight."
"We are at an altitude of 1 kilometer and descending at about 70 meters per second."
"Down to 50 meters/second, 500 meters in altitude."

At 100 meters altitude, the PDV has flown 300 meters horizontally from chute and backshell separation, ensuring its safe landing away from the shell and chute. The horizontal velocity is now brought to zero, the craft's vertical velocity is reduced to 20 meters per second.

"Engines at 90% thrust."
"Standing by for sky crane."
"Constant velocity accordion nominal, altitude error 5.9 meters."
"We found a nice, flat place, we are coming in ready for Sky Crane."
"Altitude error corrected."
"Nominal descent."
"Vertical down to 10 meters per second, 40 meters altitude."

Two hundred kilograms of the Descent Stage's two hundred ninety-eight kilograms of expected fuel consumption has been expended. To maintain a 0.75 meters per second descent rate and efficient engine operations, four engines are shutdown to 1%, and the remaining four fire at 50%, maintaining a 0.75 meters per second descent rate, the Rover landing speed at which it should meet the surface. The DS and its attached Rover descend to an altitude of 21 meters.

"Sky Crane is started."
"Descending at 0.75 meters per second as expected."
"19 meters altitude."

"PDV descent stable at 0.75 meters per second."

Rover Separation from the Descent Stage carriage initiates with its release by pyro devices. The Rover is lowered on triple bridles with a fourth umbilical cord providing power and data connection between the Rover and Descent Stage. The Rover Mobility System deploys the six wheels of the Rover as it continues to descend at 0.75 meters per second.

"Expecting bridal cut shortly."
"Signal to Odyssey remains strong."
"Signal delta nominal."
"Fuel check is good."
"Tango Delta (Touchdown) nominal."

After the initial touchdown with the Mars surface, the Rover's Inertial Measurement Unit must indicate that there is no further movement, and a stable, line of sight ultra-high frequency (UHF) decimeter band radio signal must be received from the Rover before a safe landing is assured.

"RIMU stable."
"UHF strong."
"Touchdown confirmed."
"Seven minutes, thirty-four seconds from atmospheric entry."
"We are safe on Mars."

The MSL Rover is on the surface of Mars at Gale Crater.

Within three seconds the three-cord Bridle Cut Command is sent. In less than one second the Umbilical Cord Cut Command is issued. All four connections are cut using the last four remaining pyrotechnic devices of the 76 devices used during MSL's Entry, Descent, and Landing.

Fly Away Mode initiates, and the Descent Stage hovers above the released Rover for a few additional moments. Two

MLE's power up to 100% thrust, with the remaining six at less than 80%, causing the DS to pitch over at a rapidly rising 45° angle, moving away from the landing site of the Rover named Curiosity, now settled on the surface of the planet at the bottom of Gale Grater, northwest of Aeolis Mons rising six kilometers in the distance. The remaining six engines power up to 100%, and the horizontal momentum from the pitch-over maneuver causes the vehicle to fly away from the landing site until all of the remaining propellant is consumed, with a required minimum Sky Crane impact distance to Rover of 150 meters. Eleven days later, on August 17, 2012, the High-Resolution Imaging Science Experiment camera on NASA's Mars Reconnaissance Orbiter will document that the distance of the Descent Stage Sky Crane crash site from the landed Rover was 650 meters, more than four times the minimum required distance, due to the efficiency of the landing sequence and the amount of fuel unconsumed prior to the Descent Stage flyaway.

At the time of the landing at Gale Crater, the communications distance to the Jet Propulsion Laboratory on Earth from the Rover on Mars was 13 minutes and 51 seconds. If you looked down from above the north poles onto the solar system orbits of the third and fourth planets from the sun, Earth would be at two o'clock, moving faster in its third position counterclockwise solar orbit. The fourth planet, Mars, would be at four o'clock, falling behind Earth's orbital speed due to the length of its sidereal period almost twice to that of Earth. A distance of 249 million kilometers separates the two planets.

Curiosity Rover is on the surface of Mars at Gale Crater, at 05:17 UTC, 06August2012.

In the center of the landing field, safe from the exhaust debris of the Sky Crane's descent engines sits the Curiosity Rover. The dust settles, having swirled up from the surface by the angled thrust and heat of the sky crane engine's final blast. Its marks will be erased from the surface by the effects of dust storms in the next few years. The Mars Reconnaissance Orbiter photographed the mission detritus of what items made their way to the surface after the cruise stage separated from the descent vehicle and then burned up in the atmosphere some 4,000 kilometers from the landing site. The heat shield lies on the surface, 1,400 meters behind where Curiosity rests on the surface, the backshell 550 meters beyond it, and the parachute 630 meters away. The sky crane also rests, crashed, on the Mars surface 650 meters away from the Rover where it had flown until its four titanium fuel tanks were exhausted – its final flameout, its mission to deliver the Rover the final few meters to the surface of the planet, complete.

The first Martian night approaches.
EDL Mode is complete, Sol 0 Mode Initiated.
MSL surface operations have begun.

In what seemed to the JPL Landing Team like a lifetime of almost fourteen minutes, from a distance of 249 million kilometers, the signal finally reached the Jet Propulsion Laboratory at the California Institute of Technology confirming the safe landing of Curiosity on the surface of Mars. The Team erupted in a pandemonium of cheers and applause, and an image began to scroll on the large panel EDL Live Telemetry Visualization Screen which moments before had received the streaming data from the Odyssey craft orbiting above, whose task was to relay the telemetry signals to the JPL from the rover now settled onto the surface of Gale Crater.

The rover is equipped with eight Hazard Avoidance Cameras, and four Navigation Cameras.

"Hazcam sequence has initiated. Waiting for images."
"Signal to Odyssey remains strong."
"Flight EDL images are starting to come down."

At 00:09:06 it is less than two minutes after touchdown.

"Standing by for images. Thumbnails are complete."

"It's the wheel, it's the wheel!"

"We are wheels down on Mars."

Four rows of monitors and the forty-some Landing Team members faced the image beginning to scroll down the screen which faced them, system active. Two other rooms separated by glass walls, contained other members of the JPL management and science teams, all with faces pressed against the glass, watching the LT's celebration as the image from Mars took form. The EDL Director who had singularly paced back and forth at the rear of the room during the landing sequence joined the celebration of an event now confirmed that had taken place almost fourteen minutes earlier. There had been no way of knowing what happened until the signals relayed from Curiosity to Odyssey were received on distant Earth as the sun began to set on planet Mars. It had taken nearly fourteen minutes for the signal from Mars to be received on Earth.

Looking out from the left front Hazcam, the shape of the left front wheel is half exposed along the middle of the left margin. Filling the center of the photograph, spreading before it like a dark mountain, is the shadow of the Rover, projected onto the surface by the setting sun behind it. Facing east-southeast above the expanding shadow rises Mount Sharp, Aeolis Mons, above the false horizon formed by the rim of the valley that surrounds the mountain beyond the site where Curiosity stands. Small rocks are scattered on the surface beneath the Rover's body all the way to the visible horizon which stands before the mountain. Only one rock in sight beyond Curiosity's shadow appears to be of any significant size, but still most are large enough to cast their own shadows on the surface by the light of the now more distant sun.

This is the first scene which presents itself to the Mission team, which expresses both the relief of stress and the exhilaration of success, after the final seven minutes of terror during which the spacecraft experienced atmospheric Entry to Landing, requiring a series of complex maneuvers never before attempted in order to autonomously land a spacecraft on the surface of another world. The emotions following this success are as unable to be controlled as those of a celebrating child.

There sits MSL, christened Curiosity, facing west-northwest. The setting sun illuminates the rim of Gale Crater and forms the line of the false horizon, the left rear wheel visible in the lower right corner of the picture.

This is the beginning of the surface journey, after flying through 570 million kilometers to Mars on its flight from Earth. Its planned one Martian year surface exploration, 687 Earth days, has begun. Its actual exploration will last an astounding 4,033 Earth days, equal to 3,931 Martian sols – six Martian years equal to approximately eleven Earth years. Along the way it will rediscover the ancient dreams of humankind, and when its mission ends, it will end with its nuclear heart still willing and working, but its mechanical functioning bereft of capability, finally overcome by the dust and abrasion of relentless winds. But it will not end before it can reimagine man's immortality.

The Cruise, Entry, Descent, and Landing Support team now transfers responsibility to the Surface Mission Support operations team. In the first month of surface operations, the mission will begin a four-day Characterization Activity Phase. All pyrotechnic release devices are fired to open the equipment which had been safely stowed for CEDL. Spring loaded devices are released to remove dust covers from cameras and other sensitive equipment. CAP procedures for predefined and pretested activities will be performed for instrument tests, imaging capability, electrical and thermal management related to the plutonium powered thermoelectric generator linked to lithium batteries, and the three communications antennae. Once these activities are complete, the Flight Software will be transitioned from EDL to Surface operations, with instrumentation, motor control, and mobility verification of the new software release. Scientific instrumentation, deployment, and stowage of the robotic arm will be tested for nominal science performance.

Once the execution of the sol 0-4 operations is completed in the Characterization Activity Phase, the Surface Mission Support Area teams will commence Rover activities on the surface of Mars.

v

The spacecraft which has flown hundreds of millions of kilometers from Earth has now transformed itself into a wheeled rover, emerging like a chrysalis in reverse of the metamorphosis of crawling caterpillar to flying butterfly. It first moves only a few meters away from the resting site where it landed, performs a circular maneuver, and stops to point its front Hazcam towards the direction from which it has come. It sees its own tracks in the surface dust a few centimeters deep, small rocks and pebbles littered on the flat surface it has just traversed. A three letter Morse code impression is visible in the layer of dust through which it has moved, stamped on the surface of the planet by the pattern in the rover's tread, spelling JPL, for the Jet Propulsion Laboratory which built her.

Capable of moving now at a maximum speed of one centimeter per second, it progresses only at five centimeters per ten seconds, followed by a twenty second rest to assess the location and position of the vehicle. It is traveling at a pace of about ten kilometers every one thousand days, making slow progress across the surface as it stops for dust storms, photographs, scientific experiments, and silent nights.

After one thousand five hundred sols it finally makes its way across the floor of Gale Crater to reach a land bridge enabling it to traverse the great sand dunes circling the base of Mount Aeolis, Mount Sharp.

VI
Search

i

We would not understand until later, that these sand dunes were not only the inorganic result of eons of wind erosion and endless dust storms which unceasingly pulverized the eroding rock into the powder that had the capability of stranding Curiosity in its grip. The dunes represented a constant danger to a spinning wheel which would only dig itself in deeper as if it were drowning in quicksand. The hundreds of millions of years of diatomic life cycles within the seas which once covered the surface of this third once blue planet, the fourth planet from the sun, was also the source of the powdery silicon dust, the fine black substance formed over eons as diatoms ended their life cycles and sank into the waters, creating a silky carpet of fine sediment on the bottom of the Martian seas. Now, the seas vaporized and the atmosphere long eroded, dust devils swirled on the surface, blowing this lifeless surface powder to infill every crevice on the rocky surface, and form the restless dunes over which Curiosity now rolled. The deep dunes of this fine powdery sand filled the great sea trench southwest of the landing site, surrounding the base of the volcanic mountain which had arisen from the sea bed, pierced the surface of the sea, and become the Mons in an ancient geologic history.

Having ascended Vera Rubin Ridge, Curiosity pauses to photograph its progress made thus far, looking backwards through the telephoto lens of its MastCam. After fifteen hundred days and fifteen kilometers, Curiosity has made its way across the land passage of Nathan Bridges Dune, and began to ascend the highlands beyond Ogunquit Beach. In the distance, northeast of where Curiosity stands on a rocky plain overlooking the great trench, the remains of the alluvial fan of

Peace Vallis is cratered in the rock where its water once flowed into the fresh water depths of Aeolis Palus. The floor of the volcanic crater collapsed around the edge of the center which became Aeolis Mons, Mount Sharp, the mountain within the center of the great collapsed volcanic ring now called Gale Crater.

The exposed great trench of the crater floor pointed to the southwest in the direction in which the slowly and relentlessly moving rover traversed, making its way inexorably to the Mons, somehow drawn to that point. It drew it towards itself, in a knowledge outside of what could be known, like the mysteries of the endless worlds inhabited in the sky above, a universe of stars, points of light which became unseeing eyes at night to imagine the universe, still sweeping away faster and faster in the bending motion of time and space. While it had descended from space, still enclosed blindly to sight within its back aeroshell and heatshield, MSL had passed above the Valles Marineris, deorbiting above the great Chasma of Coprates. It was once the deepest chasm, with a depth of nearly seven kilometers, in the great central ocean that covered the equatorial surface of Mars, spanning nine hundred sixty kilometers through Tharsis and Phoenicis Lacus to the desert Arabia and Sinus Sabaeus. Then flying blindly over the continuum of desert which now covered the extent of the planet's surface, its overflight had excepted only the ice-covered northern polar region of Mare Boreum and the southern polar region of Mare Australe.

For an additional 2,431 Mars sols, Curiosity will make its way across the increasingly rocky surface, as the grade increases and the ascent to the mountain begins. The fine powdery sand covering the surface is now less deep as the rocky surface slopes upwards, and the surface winds manage to fill only the crevices and leeward sides of rocks and boulders. Hazcams front and back choose the way across the surface, decided by mission control from a distance of 90 to 240 million kilometers, depending on the relative position of the two planets in their orbits. The rover pauses for photographs, measurements, scientific experiments, windstorms, and Martian nights. The winds here clear the surfaces of Curiosity more readily than when it moved through the floor of the crater. It climbs higher and higher, sol by sol, through the seasons and years etched and eroded into the surface upon which it crawls. Now it rests, still far below the summit, but it is now far above the depth of the crater and the landing site to which it had been drawn, to the space it now inhabits on the side of the mountain, drawn there like a moth, unable to fly to the flame above which would now not extinguish it.

Years before launch, the Mons held the interest of scientists, astronomers, and teams of NASA engineers. From an almost random natural selection of hundreds of sites, one crater was chosen, and the mountain that rose within. Through the ingenuity and the curiosity and the intellectual study of man, this same site would be twice chosen – for the present mission as a source of history in an attempt to understand the planet's geologic evolution with its layers of sediment from the past to the present – and as a mission in the ancient past and a repository of human history. How could we have known the doors we would discover through which man had passed and would eventually pass again? Mankind in his present consciousness had always been drawn to the planet, now red, mysteriously red.

In the intervening years after Curiosity had crossed the land passage of Nathan's Bridge, the rover would make its way to the base of this mountain, until the way was too steep or too rocky for it to continue onward and upward. On its way it would investigate layer upon layer of the rock and sediment on its upward journey, while encountering less and less dust and sand picked up from the winds in the increasingly higher elevations above the crater floor from which it had traveled. The winds scoured clean the exposed surfaces. The Rover's vertical ascension would reach a height of two kilometers from the depth of the crater landing, and the total distance traveled across the Martian surface would not exceed thirty-eight linear kilometers, a crawling pace which would span and bring together hundreds of thousands of years of human history and human dreams, in the insatiable curiosity vicariously transmitted back and forth between the machinery of the Rover and the engineers of the NASA Jet Propulsion Laboratory.

ii

What had been apparent as a star of singular reddish hue to the naked eye of early philosophers and scientists, progressed in our understanding to be a planet, not a red star, clearly visible through the polished glass lenses of early astronomers. With the development of space technology, it led to small robotic Mars landings, and then to Mars orbital vehicles capable of mapping and photographing the surface of the planet in detail. From the photographs and mappings of thousands of detailed surface structures, one hundred were chosen by international scientists for intensive and passionate debates on the merits of a landing site from which Curiosity would begin its crawl across the planet. The Mars Reconnaissance Orbiter provided additional detailed photographic and spectrographic data analytics, through the use of which the hundred sites were finally winnowed down to four.

The Eberswalde Crater exhibited evidence of ancient river channel outflows and the presence of clay deposits, a sign of surface water. Surface erosion by Mars dust storms exposed layers of clay bearing minerals.

Holden Crater appeared as one of a series of crater lakes connected by streams, as if its moving waters carved gullies and deposited sediments on now dry lakebeds, eroding some of the most ancient rock formations exposed on the surface of the planet.

Mawrth Vallis in the Oxia Palus quadrangle lies between the higher southern hemisphere and the lower northern lands, a seeming ancient channel emptying into the southern lands and containing eroded cliffs of exposed clay minerals. In fact, not to be understood until many years and explorations later, the largest northern continental river flowed through this quadrangle into the Great Southern Sea to the southwest, where lies the great sea trench, Valles Marineris.

Finally, the chosen site, Gale Crater, within which rises Aeolis Mons, Mount Sharp. Mistakenly thought to have been caused by a meteor impact some 3 1/2 billion years ago, it was in fact the site of an immense caldera-formed volcano, a massive event propelled by layered magma chambers, with a liquid lower chamber which pushed upward to release the magma and cause the emptying of its gas filled upper chamber which exploded, causing an enormous crater spanning over one hundred and forty kilometers. From the center of this crater rose the ancient mountain pushed to the surface over eons by the thrust of a new magma chamber beneath it, breaching the surface of the sea which had infilled the crater after the initial explosion. Now it was an arid and lifeless scape of winds, powder, sand, and rock; of brittle clays eroding to dust, joining the remains of trillions upon trillions upon quadrillions of cellular sea life which had lived, died, and settled to the bottom of the seas, becoming the twirling powders of dust swirls and dunes blown across the now barren surface.

And Curiosity continued its climb.

Prologue

The end was found at Aeolis Mons, Mount Sharp, on August 22, 2023, 3,931 Mars sols from the date when Curiosity landed at Gale Crater.

What was once the largest freshwater lake on the planet was now a dusty, desiccated valley, strewn with the rubble of volcanic activity alternating with areas of deep sand, the fine silica exoskeleton remains of the diatomic creatures which had inhabited the lakes and seas, lived and died and settled to the bottom in a fine black silt that if waded upon, were the water still extant, would encase the feet in a cooling paste pushing up through your feet in a satisfying soothing balm. There is no surface water now, and any evidence of it would only be found deep under the surface, not found at all were it already vaporized from the surface to escape into the thin, barren atmosphere of repeated hot, and cold, and alternating directions of the wind which the reversing temperatures generated.

From its landing site, the aptly named Curiosity Rover faced the great mountain which rose up from the valley of the crater, the target, the odyssey, the face of an improbable success of the mission, a success which would be attained beyond the imaginings of the most creative minds. It is now eleven years and sixteen Earth days since the rover landed on Mars, a scientific laboratory mission the length of which was planned and expected to function for at least only one Martian year lasting 687 Earth days – to fully experience each of the Martian seasons, including at least one Martian winter.

The mission's electrical generation was not dependent on sweeping clear solar panels in order to provide continuous electrical power. A plutonium fueled thermoelectric generator with five kilograms of Plutonium238 radioactive metal provided a powered assurance to recharge its lithium-ion batteries despite dust clouds or sunny days, temperatures high or low. Now on its 4,033rd Earth day, the Morse Code of Curiosity's wheels are perforated to the point of imminent failure, the exposed surfaces of all metallic parts are polished to an opalescent patina by eleven Earth years of unending wind and dust storms. It has slowly made its way up the mountain like an Alpinist reaching to secure a last anchor, before exhaustion threatens to turn back the climber.

The plutonium energy source which provided electricity, heat, and life to the machine has made this ironically possible. The nuclearization, where man had begun anew and then ended, made this possible through the technology which temporarily bridled its power. We were somehow drawn again to find this new, now old, barren world, once the second Eden. Lost, abandoned, forgotten, it was inaccessible for two hundred millenniums until man learned once again to free himself from the bonds of the Earth and moon's orbit, and escape the destruction of his terrible knowledge. In the coming years after Curiosity's mission and the discovery it made on Aeolis Mons, and after the MSL's twin rover – Mars 2020 Perseverance – confirmed the earlier presence of water at Jezero Crater, a manned exploration would return to the now desolate planet to begin an exploration of the structure within the Mons. Gradually over many years, eight of the pure silicone dioxide quartz boules would be rediscovered and understood – the four boules deeply archived within the Mons, and one each at quadrangles Ismenius, Iapygia, Coprates, and Phaethontis – still sealed within each the ancient record of life on Earth, life that had escaped from the massive Uinkaret volcanic event of double ages past. Only the ninth boule, which had been accessible for use as a searchable database at the Mars settlement on the banks of Lake Aeolis, was unknown and lost. Discoveries of the new explorers would include the orbital description inscribed on the surface of each quartz vessel which depicted the path of the ancient Earth-launched spacecraft still orbiting the sun, with cryogenically preserved life still contained viably within, completing its three thousand eight hundredth journey around the sun, each a one hundred five Earth-year orbit.

In further years to come, a robotic vehicle would capture and bring back to Earth this ancient spacecraft still orbiting between the seventh and eighth planets, which held the record of man's first life on Earth, and by the time of that year in which this discovery would be made, there would be enough understanding of the human genome to interpret the first age of man and how its genetic remains still populate the cells of every present-day human. A further understanding of what it meant to be human, a new depth of humanity which had waited to be rediscovered after hundreds of millennia, a briefest history of time in the current ancient but still expanding universe. Of how many preceding universes and their ultimate event horizons were escaped by our conscious ancestries, we would only be able to imagine.

But what can be imagined within our own present universe can be done. What was done can be reimagined. The present record still remains, unbroken from launch-to-launch since the eleventh Marine Isotope Stage four hundred thousand years ago and across two worlds until the present time, from world to world, however it is that you define the present day of the future, and the beginnings of the past. We will never attain the future world, as the present stretches out before us. Only the past is what we are left to remember. The definition of life is what is contained in our DNA and in the DNA of all living things.

Perhaps the greatest puzzle can never be known, when our entire universe ceases to expand and collapses unto itself, to begin again from the gravitational singularity of a new 35-billion-year cycle. Will all be lost to begin again at the edge of that cataclysmic event horizon, to which all time and space will have returned? Will some memory in the DNA of our life remain to arise again in the instant after the new inevitable beginning? Male to female, haploid to diploid, world to world, galaxy to galaxy, in a universe of expanding and collapsing space and time, of living and dying, and living again, the essence of life and the consciousness to reimagine and rediscover it all anew. After all, and in the end, is the prologue the true epilogue?

Perhaps all will not be lost, only paused to be reconstituted and remembered within our cells, and reborn without a conscious knowledge of the past or the future. Perhaps the great scientist was correct when he considered man's ability to understand a universe in which he was able to perceive himself, that "God is sophisticated, but he is not malicious." What remains is the individual unattainable future as the present stretches out before us in space and time, unending until the ending.

And then the new beginning.

Out of the darkness.

Light.

Ж